good girls

pole riders club

good girls

pole riders club

a novel

KIMONA JAYE

ATRIA BOOKS
NEW YORK   LONDON
TORONTO   SYDNEY

ATRIA BOOKS

A Division of Simon & Schuster, Inc.
1230 Avenue of the Americas
New York, NY 10020

First Atria Books trade paperback edition January 2008

ATRIA BOOKS and colophon are trademarks of Simon & Schuster, Inc.

For information about special discounts for bulk purchases, please contact Simon & Schuster
Special Sales at 1-800-456-6798 or business@simonandschuster.com.

Manufactured in the United States of America

10 9 8 7 6 5 4 3 2 1

The Library of Congress has cataloged the hardcover edition as follows:
Good girls pole riders club: a novel / Kimona Jaye.
    p. cm.
    1. African American women—Fiction. 2. Female friendship—Fiction.
3. Stripteasers—Fiction. I. Title.
PS3610.A96G66 2007
813'.6—dc22   2006047863
ISBN-13: 978-0-7432-9202-3

ISBN-13: 978-0-7432-9210-8 (pbk)

To all of my girls and fellow pole riders everywhere: may nothing obscure your sky or cut off your air. Like it's hot, baby!

good girls

pole riders club

1

We made a pact. Not for our men, but for ourselves, really. The five of us would buy a pole. A stripper's pole—mirror-finished stainless steel, attached from floor to ceiling. It was approaching midnight, and we had already polished off two shakers of chocolate-banana martinis. Shaundra was on the couch. Me and Niecee sat on either side of the coffee table; Brenda was on the love seat, half passed out after one drink, as usual. Karina was wide awake, with sweats on, legs positioned in an overextended V as she stretched her open palm toward her toes. The idea was Shaundra's. Had anyone else come up with it, we would have laughed it off and moved on to the next thing. But Shaundra was grounded. She wasn't nasty like Niecee, who was willing to try anything once, and she wasn't scary like Brenda. She was our middle mark. We measured ourselves by her, usually without even knowing it. Everyone else was too skinny, too fat, too loud, too quiet, and too loose—all by Shaundra's position in our crew.

"I'm gonna cut it off. Clean off, I swear," Shaundra said.

"Ohh, nooo. You're in love, remember. He just treats you sooo wonderful and he's sooo attentive." Niecee smirked, stirred her electric-blue nail around the inside of her martini glass, then sucked her entire middle finger into her mouth.

"Why are you always tryin'ta catch somebody with their own words?"

Niecee swirled her tongue around her finger one good time, then pointed it at Shaundra. "Don't get mad at me because you were chasing his stank drawers last week. It ain't my fault you *luvs* him." Niecee smiled, then whipped her hard-pressed hair from her shoulder to her back.

"Let her talk, Niecee," I interjected.

"Shay, why don't you concentrate on taking those horsehair braids out of your head. You're almost done."

She whipped her hair again for good effect. Niecee was cute and she knew it—milk chocolate, in good shape, with her real hair cutting almost to the middle of her back.

I continued unbraiding the middle of my head. "All I have to say is *don't fall asleep*, cuz all your shit might be cut off when you wake up."

"That's what I said," Shaundra started up again. "I'ma cut his shit straight off. Let me find another stripper's number in his pants."

"How do you know it's a stripper's number?" Karina asked as she tucked her right leg into her overly thick thigh for another stretch.

"She gave him a business card." Shaundra reached across the coffee table into her purse.

"That's a shame. Even strippers have business cards nowadays." I shook my head. "Maybe I should get some made up: *Housewife seeks adventure—will pay you.*" She handed me the stripper's card. I flipped to the back and then to the front again.

"Brit-ten-ney. The girl doesn't even know how to spell," Shaundra said.

The card was glossy, printed on a nicely weighted cardstock. *Brittenney—Petite Goddess* was printed at the top left of the card, and a photograph of a light-skinned young woman with a long black weave and pouted lips was on the right. She had a deer-in-the-headlights, wide-eyed look on her face, her left hand draped the bare skin above her braless breast, and her nipples were cropped off the card by a black border.

I passed the card to Karina. "'*Actress, Exotic Dancer, Escort, Private Parties. Call for rates.*' What does *incall/outcall* mean?"

Niecee took another sip of her drink. "It means his place or hers."

I shot Karina a look. She placed the card on the table. "Well," she said, "it still doesn't mean he's into strippers. He could have gotten that card anywhere."

Shaundra plucked her glass from the coffee table and adjusted her feet again under the purple afghan. "I know he's into strippers, and I'm tired of him telling me that the government is garnishing his check for child support."

"Well, Shaundra, that isn't so far-fetched," I said, wanting to comfort her.

She threw up her hands and rolled her eyes to the back of her head. "Are you sleeping with him too now?"

I rolled my eyes in rebuttal. "I'm just saying, Shaun."

"I have seen his pay stub and talked to his ex-wife." Shaundra pursed her lips. "He's *not* getting garnished; he's giving his money to Cotton Candy and Honey Dip."

Niecee flicked her hair again. "You know you need the hickory stick as much as he needs the *na-na*. Stop complaining."

I grabbed a pile of unbraided hair from my hair bag and threw it at her. Sometimes I just wanted to strangle Niecee. We'd been friends since junior high — well, not really. Brenda, Shaundra, Karina, and I were friends. Niecee was Shaundra's older sister and roommate, so we tolerated her for those two reasons alone.

"I may as well share this with y'all now. You're gonna find out anyway." Shaundra sat up straight, knocked the purple afghan from her lap, and smoothed her hands over her stretched-to-the-max size 13 blue denim jeans. "I'm ordering a pole."

"You're ordering a what?" Brenda uncurled her five-foot-ten-inch body from the fetal position she had been in on the love seat.

"I thought you were asleep," I said.

"You must be talking about a fishing pole, right?" Karina asked, looking up from one of the three *Travel & Leisure* magazines spread between her stretched legs.

"She's talking about a booty clap, come-fuck-me-for-a-ten-spot pole."

"Is that how much you used to charge, Niecee?"

"Ooohhhh!" we all cooed. Shaundra rarely stood up to Niecee. I reached over to Shaundra and high-fived her, then held up my hand to Niecee for another high five. She left me hanging.

"Please"—she flicked her hair—"I only did that for a week. And it was good money."

"I'm ordering a stripper's pole," Shaundra confessed. "And I was thinking"—a devious grin spread on her lips—"maybe y'all want to go in with me."

"You can't be serious," Karina said before I could get the words out.

A part of me was thrilled. The other part felt like I had entered an alternate universe. This was different, even for us.

"Well, I'm in," Brenda said matter-of-factly. "Just let me know how much and I'll get you a check this week."

"Shaun, you're really getting a stripper's pole?" I asked.

"Why not? I'm a good woman. Why should I lose my man to someone just because she knows how to shake her behind and wrap her leg around a pole? Way I see it, I need to join the game."

"Well, I'm down, too," Niecee said, "as long as I can pay you in weekly installments."

We all looked at her.

"What?" She sat up on her knees and poured the last of the martinis into her glass. "I'm not balling like y'all. Twenty-five dollars a week is better than nothin'. Besides, I could stand a little practice."

"Karina? Shay?" Shaundra looked at us both. "Are y'all in?"

Karina waved both of her hands above her head. "Nunh-uh, y'all. It's taken me a year and a half to get down to my weight. I'm not gonna mess around and risk a broken hip because I was swinging my fat butt on a pole. Besides, I'd have to pray about it anyway."

"Here we go," Niecee said under her breath.

"Shay?"

I looked at Shaundra. "So I guess we'd have it one week a month or something like that?"

"Whoop, whoop! Okay, you're in." I hadn't seen Shaundra this excited since she found out she was pregnant with Brandi. "We can each get the pole for one week, from Saturday to Saturday. I already picked one out. It's stainless steel, splits in two pieces, and comes with its own carrying case. We won't even have to drill holes or anything."

"So, how much?" Brenda leaned forward on the love seat.

"Five hundred forty dollars and eleven cents. If we split it four ways, that'll be a hundred and thirty-five apiece, a reasonable investment in our relational and sexual futures." Shaundra ran her hand over her recently cropped hair. "It's hardball time now. If Paul wants a stripper, from this point on, he'll have sistah Good-n-Plenty at home."

"Amen, sistah. 'Bout time you got some sense."

Everyone starred at Niecee again.

She bucked her eyes. "That's real. If a broad handles her own business, she ain't got to worry about another heffa doing it for her." She swept her tongue around the rim of her glass.

Her words struck a chord of truth inside of me. "This is a trip. We are really going to do this stripper-pole time-share thing. I would have never believed it."

"Does it come with an instructional tape?" Brenda asked in her most intellectual voice.

Niecee jumped in. "What are you gonna learn from a tape? You have to get this experience the natural way, at a strip club. You pick it up as it comes. And that's easier for *some* of us than it is for *others*." She smirked at Brenda, her right dimple deepening to its fullest. Brenda was never very rhythmic; that hadn't changed since junior high.

"Brenda, you could catch on if you really wanted to. Don't even listen to Niecee. Besides"—Shaundra let her own right dimple deepen—"I'm going down to the club this Saturday. If y'all want to come, you're welcome to roll."

"I'll ride," Niecee said. "I might run into one of my old girls."

"I'm down, too," Brenda said, ignoring Niecee's chuckle.

Karina rolled her ankles to finish off her stretching and closed her magazine. "I'm gonna have to talk to the Man Upstairs about this, but I think y'all are gonna need a prayer warrior in the house, so tentatively count me in."

I was the only one left. I wanted to go, but I knew Mark was going to flip out more about the club than he would about the pole or me having an occasional drink with my crew now and then. "Y'all my girls, but I don't know. I've already hung with y'all once this week; I might be pushing it."

"Why don't you just spit the truth, *Shoshannah*." Niecee winked at me and it irked the hell out of me. "You'se got to ask Minister Mark. And Lord knows, Minister Mark don't want his wife hanging out in no den of sin. Heavens no."

"Leave her alone, Niecee. Ain't nothing wrong with trying to be a good Christian wife. Shay ain't got nothing to be ashamed of." Karina gave me a glance of approval.

Niecee rolled her eyes. "Good Christian *what?* Please. Y'all can live in la-la land if you want to, but she's probably the biggest sinner of all of us. The innocent-looking ones are always the worst k—"

"You need to worry about yourself. We all know hell's got a special spot waiting for your scandalous butt," Brenda said, still mad about the insinuation that she didn't have rhythm.

Niecee giggled, then smoothed her palm over her hair slowly. "There's a whole wing waiting for my ass, 'cause I don't half-do nothin'."

I grabbed my week-old blush Shiseido glasses from the table, then collected the stray extensions from my lap and most of the ones I had thrown at Niecee. Cautiously, I lifted myself up from the ground, feeling the slightest bit tipsy. "Shaundra, I'm gonna head home, but don't worry, I've got your back Saturday night."

2

At 1:35 A.M., I pulled into the garage feeling like a guilty teenager. Mark always left the garage door up when he knew I'd be in late, but he seldom stayed up to wait on me. He would be asleep already, I knew that, but the idea of him finding out I went to a strip club made me more anxious than normal. I grabbed the trial-size Crest tube, mouthwash, and hand towel I stowed away in the door pocket of my SUV. After applying the toothpaste to my teeth and tongue, I cupped my hands over my mouth and blew twice. All I'd had to drink was one Long Island iced tea, but I could still smell a tinge of alcohol. I couldn't tell if it was the vodka, tequila, rum, or gin that was giving me away. It didn't help that Shaundra poured her London Fog down my pants. She *thought* she spotted Paul, her man, on the other side of the club. He was supposed to be working the night shift.

Shaundra dropped her face in my lap like a hot biscuit. I guess it didn't occur to her that she had a full drink in her hand. The ice and chilled alcohol formed a pool in my crotch, then seeped through my pants into what little there was of my brand-new, stripper-inspired, purple net, lace-up-on-both-sides panties. I could see it wasn't Paul, even without my glasses. Instead of trying to grab a few napkins, all Niecee could talk about was how Shaundra just threw away seven dollars. I could still hear the sassy, singsong sound of Niecee's voice in my head, "And you better be glad we *didn't* go to the Fish Pond. That drink would have cost you nine dollars there. Damn shame. That's alcohol abuse." Wasted liquor was one of Niecee's true pet peeves. It brought out the conservationist in her. She didn't recycle glass bottles or aluminum, she didn't have her groceries bagged in paper instead of plastic, and she wasn't trying to save the ozone layer by not spraying aerosols. But when it came to alcohol, she never wanted to see a good drink go to waste.

Despite the wetness from the spill, once I got over the instant freeze in my crotch, I still couldn't bring myself to go to the bathroom. I just stood up slightly to coax the excess liquid from my lap, then sat my jacket down under me to give me something dry to sit on. This was my first time in a strip club, and confident black woman that I am, I didn't want to move or draw attention to myself. None of us did—besides Niecee. Niecee had on what I like to call her "sausage call" dress. It was too tight, too short, and too low-cut. She had pounded, pulled, and prayed 145 pounds worth of legs, breasts, and butt into a tube of yellow spandex fit for a size 2 anorexic and accessorized her ensemble with glass stilettos.

Though the club seemed fairly new, the walls and furnishings were saturated with cigarette smoke. In the center of the club was a long Plexiglas stage with two poles on each end, both ascending high into the warehouse-height ceiling. Men on metal barstools lined both sides of the stage, and four seats flanked the front. Alcohol and dollar bills were abundant.

We sat in the back, in the farthest booth from the stage. We were five of nine women in the club who weren't strippers. Our male counterparts flanked us to the north, east, and west; a paneled glass mirror flanked us from behind.

"Girl," Niecee said loudly into the atmosphere of R. Kelly grind-music and testosterone. "I just love the smell of men." She spoke from the last seat of our horseshoe-shaped booth. She sat with her legs a knee's width apart and wiggled the tips of her fingers toward the backs of the men. "Makes me want to hop myself on the stage and leave you prudes here to dry. Y'all sitting in the back like nobody can see you."

Niecee placed her drink onto one of the small table surfaces built into our booth, faced the stage, and commenced to get her groove on. Her bare, brown arms made loose waves above her head. Her hips gyrated in deep ovals.

"I don't know why we needed to come all the way down here to learn anything. Look at your sister." I pointed. Niecee continued the deep ovals and made her way to her feet. She and the barely clad chocolate Pocahontas on the stage seemed to have a thing going.

"Girl, stop her!" Karina said, leaning in toward Shaundra and grabbing her free arm. "Brothas are starting to look back here at us."

"Ain't you just thirty?" Niecee shouted back over her shoulder at Karina. She moved into the empty space in front of our horseshoe, where a table would have been if we weren't in a strip club with built-ins. "You sound like an old-ass lady."

"Hurry up and sit down!" Karina demanded.

She didn't sit down. She and Pocahontas matched each other move for move. Chocolate Pocahontas squatted down; Niecee squatted down. Pocahontas groped her fringed breasts and wiggled them around; Niecee wiggled hers around. Pocahontas leaned forward toward the row of men in front of her, rested her fingertips on the Plexiglas stage, and let the expanse of her behind roll a slow grind against the black pole. Niecee widened her legs into a healthy V and commenced to bend over.

A combination of "whoo-whoops," claps, and laughter exploded from the audience. Some men concentrated on Pocahontas, others on Niecee, but most, unable to choose, looked like they were watching a heated Wimbledon match.

"Ew, girl, this is embarrassing," I whispered into Shaundra's shoulder. "Why does your sister have a canary-yellow G-string on under her dress? Uh-oh. This is too wrong." A flash of heat flooded my cheeks. Niecee had broken out into a deep booty shake, and I found myself almost impressed by how she made her butt cheeks slap together like that.

"She's grown," is all Shaundra managed to say. She sat with

her back board-straight and sipped methodically on her London Fog as she watched Niecee's behind bounce up and down.

"Girl, I hate to say this"—Karina pressed her index and middle finger against her neck to monitor her heart rate—"but I'm glad that that's your sister and not mine, because I would have to kick her natural-born a-s-s. I ain't lyin'. All five of my toes and my ankle would be lodged somewhere between her behind and her throat. Lord, forgive me for my language," she managed to say as an afterthought.

Brenda didn't say anything, but I could tell she wanted to. She had been the consummate butt of Niecee's jokes for so many years, her distaste for Niecee had turned into a distinguishable hate.

"Whew. Hand me a napkin, would you?" Niecee said, plopping back into her end seat. She adjusted her dress. Everyone looked at each other, then finally Karina handed her one. "Thank you, girl, that was a workout and a half. Umph, it's been too long."

"Clearly *not* long enough," Brenda interjected.

Niecee wiped her forehead, then between her breasts. "You're just jealous because I have mad sex appeal and you don't." She didn't bother to look at Brenda. She merely pulled a damp twenty from her bra and waved it in the air.

A twentysomething, honey-toned girl wearing a metallic silver string bikini with matching thigh-high boots came over to her. Niecee whispered something in her ear.

"You sure?" the girl said, her hand propped above her gluteus minimus.

Niecee nodded, "Girl, yeah, but I'll catch you next time."

"As long as you're sure." The girl caressed Niecee's cheek and walked away.

Within moments, I saw Pocahontas making her way from the rear exit toward our section.

"I do not believe this," popped from my mouth. It took me a few seconds to recognize the sound of my own voice. I squeezed Brenda's leg hard. Shaundra squeezed mine. Karina closed her eyes for what I'm sure was a silent prayer.

"You want it here or in the back?" Pocahontas said with a Brooklyn drawl, leaning her 36Ds into Niecee's face.

Niecee looked at Pocahontas, then back over at us. "You better take me in the back 'cause these prudes ain't gonna mess up my flow. Shaundra, since you tryin' to learn some shit, you might wanna get a lap dance yourself. But that's your business." Niecee flicked her hair, then stood up. If not for the stilettos, she and Pocahontas would have been eye to eye.

Pocahontas grinned. "Am I giving you one or are you doing me?"

Niecee grabbed moccasin girl's hand and placed it on her behind. "We'll take turns. Later, heffas. You better not leave me, Shaundra."

"Uggh! Your sister is nasty!" I said as we watched her trail off toward the rear exit. I looked in the direction of the doorway much longer than I was supposed to. Something existed on that side of life that didn't exist in mine. This was the first time I'd ever felt jealous of Niecee.

"Is it safe for her to go back there?" Shaundra asked with a steady eye on the doorway Niecee had disappeared through.

"Safe for who?" Brenda asked irritably. "The stripper?"

Shaundra laughed slightly but held her gaze. I held mine as well. "I don't know who I should worry about more." She laughed again.

"Karina, watch my purse." Brenda snapped her change pouch, rezipped her purse, then placed it behind Karina's back.

"Something ain't right," I mumbled to Shaundra. "Brenda, baby girl, where do you think you're going?"

Brenda straightened her slender, five-foot-ten, red-and-black-clad, Olive Oyl–esque frame. A folded twenty-dollar bill was clipped tightly between her thumb and index finger. "I'm getting a lap dance. Does anyone here have a problem with that?" She folded her arms over her bony chest and eyed each of us with defiant awkwardness.

"No, Officer Brent. No problem at all. Handle yours."

• • •

It was Mark calling my name and tapping his knuckle gently on the Navigator's smoked glass window that brought me back.

"*Shoshannah. Shoshannah.*"

I clicked the key forward in the ignition, then rolled the window down.

"Oh, I'm sorry, honey, I didn't hear you walk up. Did I disturb your sleep?"

I stared at Mark's face. His eyes had the glazed-over look of just waking up.

"Shoshannah, you have to call when you know you're coming in really late. Don't make me get out of bed looking for you."

I glanced at the car clock: 2:21. I had told Mark that I would be home just after midnight.

"I'm so sorry, honey. I got in just after one. I think I just dozed off." I stuck my hand out of the window and motioned for Mark's hand. He limply joined his hand to mine and groped his hairless chin with the other.

"That's not good enough, Shannah, and you know it. I'm a pastor now; I'm in my own church. Money is short and I'm under heavy pressure to build the membership. Pressure is high, baby. I don't need my wife adding to the pot. You are supposed to be my helpmate." He looked me in the eye. "You have to work with me, not against me, dear."

"You're right, Marcus. I'm sorry."

Now that he had given his customary "helpmate" speech, he tightened his hold on my hand. "It's okay. I forgive you. Just next time, ask yourself, 'What would Jesus do?' And we both know that Jesus would have called home."

I gave an obligatory nod.

"Are you coming in?" he asked.

"In a minute, I'm just gonna clean out the car first. I dropped a crumbcake muffin earlier."

"All right. I might be asleep by the time you finish your shower. Was dinner good?"

"It was fine. Shaundra is really excited about her promotion. Eight years at the electric company is a long time."

"I guess that's why you put on a little makeup, huh?"

"I put on makeup because I wanted to, Marcus. African Methodist Episcopalian women can wear makeup, honey. It's my right."

He kissed my hand. "You just look better without it." He squeezed.

"It's still my right, Marcus."

"I know, just like you hanging out in smoky restaurants with your heathen girlfriends. The only decent one is Karina. But let's not start. You've known them since junior high—I know, I know. I'll just have to keep praying for us."

He hit the super-duper, two-dimpled grin that made me drop my guard and go out on a date with him twelve years ago.

"And I guess I have to pray for us, too." I gave a limp half smile.

"Well, if I pray hard enough, maybe I'll have my wife with me at church tomorrow. It's my first communion in my own congregation; I'd love for you to be there to take part. You're the first lady now. Must feel pretty good, huh?"

"Yeah," I said, lying to the both of us. I wasn't the first-lady type. Marcus knew that before he married me. "We'll see about tomorrow, Marcus. I promised Brenda I'd help her with her yard sale."

"Well, think about it, and if God puts it on your heart, I'm leaving at six-thirty. Sharp."

I nodded and watched him walk barefoot back into the house, all the while wondering if Brenda's yard sale was this Sunday or the next.

3

"Please come to order, the Honorable Cecil E. Gibson is now presiding. No talking, please . . ."

Standing on the courtroom floor in a tan long-sleeved shirt, size 4 olive green pants, seven-point-star badge over her heart, and 9mm handgun on her right hip, she had said the same saying over 15,000 times during the last nine years of her life. She could say it backward. Call the court to order while at the same time formulating her grocery list in the back of her head. She knew every expectation of her job. Seems like she could just look at a plaintiff or a defendant and see they were going to be trouble before they ever opened their mouth in front of the judge. It was her job to sense; it was her job to know, but to follow up her knowing with proof before she acted.

And that's what she had done last Saturday night: followed up her knowing with proof. She tested herself and found something she wanted. Something that wasn't sure and strait-laced, something that wouldn't make her parents proud. It was just for her, no one else.

Brenda had followed Niecee's example. She had grabbed a twenty-dollar bill from her purse and made her way to the rear doorway. The guard was a brother. He stared at her. Looked Brenda up and down.

"I'd like a dance. A private one."

He kept his arms crossed over his chest and gave her the once-over again. "What kind of favors you looking for, Slim? Let me guess—you want the girl with the longest tongue, right? That's Star, and she'll take care of your ass for seventy-five."

Part of being a peace officer is never letting someone throw you. Never looking out of place or like you don't have things under control. Brenda didn't have anything under control. She looked him in the eye and uncupped her hand to reveal the moist twenty-dollar bill in her palm.

He looked down, then rolled his eyes. "Frank," he called over his shoulder, "get Mackie to give this lesbo five minutes."

She didn't challenge him or throw a smirk on her face. She didn't even speak. She let him take control, something her police training had taught her never to do.

The room was the size of a small walk-in closet. It was dark and moist, like the inside of a gym shoe after someone has run five miles. It smelled like one as well. On the wall, to the side of the love seat, was a plug-in freshener that coated the warm flesh-on-flesh air with a mist of spiced orange. Same kind she kept in her bathroom at home, she thought.

Brenda sat on the edge of the love seat and stared around the room. It wasn't like she expected fresh flowers and paintings on the walls or anything, but the walls were blank and lumpy, like if she peeled back the black paint, she'd hit several coats of other equally drab colors. When Mackie walked in, the neon light coated her body in a wash of blue. Brenda reached forward in an attempt to hand her the twenty-dollar bill.

"You pay afterward," the girl said, walking over to the CD player on the wall and pressing play. She turned back toward her and began to undo the bow around her neck. The silver strings fell. She reached around her back and pulled the rear strings to make the rest of it fall. Mackie moved toward Brenda; she cocked her right leg on the couch so that her metallic crotch was directly in front of her. Brenda started to turn away and Mackie realigned Brenda's focus with her hand.

"Look at it," she said, watching her watch it. "I want you to see exactly what you are making wet."

Mackie pressed her fingertips into Brenda's shoulders and

gently pushed her back into the stale velvet love seat, then placed both of her hands on the inside of Brenda's thighs. She pulled Brenda's legs apart and pushed her French-cut-bikini-covered behind into Brenda's crotch. Brenda felt paralyzed from the legs down. She groped the fine hairs of the couch with her left hand and kept her right hand tightly clenched around the balled-up twenty.

"I haven't had a virgin in a minute," she said, grabbing both of Brenda's hands and placing them on her breasts. Mackie's breasts were warm. Almost hot. Moist. As soon as Brenda's hands fell away, Mackie caught them and placed them back.

"You ain't got to be afraid of me—I only bite if you want me to. Rub them breasts, girl. Don't it feel good?"

Brenda didn't say yes; she didn't say no. It felt awkward for her to touch another woman's breasts. It seemed normal for Mackie to have hers touched. Mackie let loose. Her metallic behind moved up and down and round and round between Brenda's legs. She made noises. She bit her own lip. Her body writhed as she forced her flesh into Brenda's. Brenda closed her eyes.

"You like it, don't you?"

Brenda didn't even know how to answer. She rubbed Mackie's breasts as methodically as she would rub her own if she were pleasuring herself.

"You like it," Mackie said, her voice sounding guttural and aroused. "Your pussy is wet, isn't it?" Mackie loosed one hand from around Brenda's neck. "Answer me," she said as her free hand made it to Brenda's waistband. "If you don't answer, I'm gonna have to check for myself."

Sensations exploded from every part of Brenda's body. She wanted to speak; she didn't know what to say. YES was too much of a commitment. NO was a lie. Brenda wiggled as Mackie's hand made it under her waistband and into her panties. Mackie cupped hair and flesh in her backward-turned hand. She was on the spot. Mackie pressed.

"Yes," Brenda let out in a shudder. She could feel Mackie's smile, but she couldn't see her face. And then, when the music changed to signal five minutes had elapsed, on cue, Mackie hit cool-down mode. She pulled her hand out of Brenda's pants. The gyrations lost their force and became loose rivulets. Her arm lost its hold around Brenda's neck. The show was over.

"Next visit, I'll give you extra time," Mackie whispered into Brenda's perspiring neck before she got up to retrieve her bikini top from the floor and exited the room.

Brenda sat on the couch dazed, wanting a tissue or something to wipe the moisture from her body. Now she felt warm all over and exposed. She would give herself a moment to recover, and then she would walk out of the room pretending. She would pretend that nothing spectacular had happened to her. She would act as though one lap dance would do it for her for the rest of her life. But already, she knew. She didn't want Mackie or think of her as beautiful. She loved Mackie's power and freedom and she wanted it for herself.

That night when Brenda got home, she closed her eyes and played the tape of the lap dance over again in her mind. And this time she imagined that Mackie was her customer. This time, when the music changed, it was Brenda who took the sweaty twenty-dollar bill from the couch and stuck it in her crotch.

4

Being a stay-at-home wife, with no children, I counted on Shaundra's calls throughout the day. Nine months earlier, Mark and I had moved from the 1,132-square-foot home we'd lived in for six years into a house double the size, twenty miles from our old neighborhood. I loved our new house; it was in a brand-new development, and we'd picked out everything from the carpet to the kitchen tile and countertops.

Some of my time was spent reading romance novels I usually bought at the grocery store, but most of it was spent cooking, cleaning, and decorating. By the end of the year, it was my goal to make sure each room, hallway, and alcove had a polished touch. I liked that, Mark giving me control of the place pretty much without question, but sometimes the silence in the house made me crazy. In general, Regal Crest felt like Rose Hills Cemetery in terms of the neighborhood tempo. The women, for the most part, weren't June Cleavers; many of them had careers and left nannies to home-make and take their children to the park during the day. I was the non-mother, non-career anomaly and I missed being able to drive five or ten minutes to Shaundra's or Brenda's house whenever I felt like it.

I always got the idea, however, that Marcus liked the separation. If you were to think of our old house, Brenda's house, and Shaundra's all being on one line, ours was the farthest east, Shaun's was the farthest west, and Brenda's was somewhere in the middle. We had lived in Laneside, an old neighborhood that was quickly getting gentrified because of its proximity to the airport and the only public golf course for over thirty miles. Our old neighborhood was a mix of young white and black couples, with a few older black couples and widows who refused to sell. Brenda lived in Greenside, but my girls and I called it Oldsville. I didn't think what had happened in our old neighborhood just blocks away was ever going to happen there. Most of her neighbors had been living in these houses since they were built and clearly intended to die in them. Brenda was one of the few second-generation owners and held to the same aesthetic of manicured lawns and neighborhood watch as they did.

Though Shaundra's neighborhood had been the cream-of-the-crop place to live only thirty years before because of the size of the lots and the palatial single-story homes, the neighborhood had taken a turn for the worse over the last ten years. Besides Workman and St. Bart's, if you wanted to score some crack or weed, this was definitely the place to do it. Shaundra barely let Brandi go outside by herself because it was impossible to tell if the young boys trying to spit game at her teenage daughter were drug dealers or normal teenagers. The uniform for all of them was the same—white XL T-shirt, baggy jeans, and cap.

I had been standing at the sink, drying dishes and thinking about my situation, when Shaundra's call popped me back into reality.

"Hey, Momma," I said into the phone.

Her pitch was a little higher than a whisper, but I could hear the enthusiasm. "Go to your computer, I want to show you something."

"I'm drying dishes."

"Shay, hurry up. My break is almost over."

I tossed my drying rag on the counter. "What?" I said, waking the computer from sleep mode.

"Okay, okay, go to www.stripclass.com."

"Shaundra, are you going through the change of life or something? You have us buying poles and going to strip clubs; I am not taking a stripper class."

"Shut up, Shay, and go the to the class schedule. They have a

Pole 101 and Body Beautiful class offered tonight. Which one are we going to?"

I got up from the computer and walked back into the kitchen. "You are on your own."

"Shay, I know you are not gonna leave me hanging. Six or seven o'clock?"

I rested my back against the sink's tiled edge. "No, Shaun. You are going to get me in trouble. You know Mark would shit his pants."

Her voice got lower, but more intense. "You are really tripping, Shay. Do you think Mark is going to be mad at you because you're learning techniques to spice up *his* sex life? Preachers need love too."

She made me laugh. "You are silly. How much?"

"Unh-huh. I knew you wanted to go. Thirty bucks a class if we pay at the door."

"I haven't even gotten my braids redone yet, and I'm out of contact solution, so I would have to wear my glasses." I fingered the pink and black bandanna scarf on my head. My hair was a mess: still ridge-lined because I'd had the braids in for so long, and my ends needed clipping badly.

"Put it in a ponytail. I'm leaving work early; I'll pick you up at five-fifteen. Bye."

Pole Dance 101 was more than a notion. At least for me anyway. A short, cute, white girl around twenty-three with a waist around the same size, taught the class. Shaundra and I arrived early to the one-room studio and inadvertently walked in on a hot and heavy lap dancing class that was still in session. Casey, the same instructor who was to teach our 101 class, invited us in to pick out our shoes while we waited for class to begin.

Shaundra and I, wearing our high school gym class attire — sweats and a T-shirt — shuffled across the floor passing eight girls, most of them in booty shorts and a tank top, one in a corset, doing what I would later find out was called *the frog* on one another's laps.

"I can't believe I let you drag me out to a damn stripping class, Shaun." I pinched her arm and then hung on to it as we started giggling.

"I can't believe it either. I think I'm a little scared, girl," she said.

"Me too," but I was more exhilarated than anything. "For real though, thank you, Shaundra. I haven't even stepped on the floor yet and I just feel . . . alive. Like I have never done anything more exciting in my life. High five for that." Our hands clasped in the air and we started giggling again.

The shoe rack was filled with about twenty-five pairs of platform pumps of various sizes with heels ranging from four to six inches. Shaundra picked up a size ten with a clear platform heel and black leather straps.

"Be sure to pick a pair a half size smaller than your normal size," the instructor yelled across the room. I found a pair of four-inch heels with iridescent white leather and laced them on my feet. I grew from five-six to five-ten and my knees knocked together the first time I tried to step. I walked around a little to try to get my bearings.

Our class consisted of five girls, including Shaun and me, and the instructor. Because there were only three poles in the studio, Casey made us pick a partner other than the person we came with and split time doing the techniques on the pole.

We started off with simple walking. Casey explained that a good stripper walk was all in balancing our weight properly in our hips, making a diagonal across the body with our feet, while dragging the toes and keeping one leg straight while popping the hip. Nothing sounded too complicated, but doing all that at the same time, I expected to have some problems. I looked across the room and gave Shaundra an "I hope I don't fall flat on my face" look.

Shaundra looked comfortable, like she couldn't wait for Casey to let her out of the gate. I always liked that about her, how she always looked at home in her own skin. Next to Karina, Shaundra was the second biggest member of our group. Niecee was the most in shape, and Brenda was the tallest and the skinniest. I was in the middle, not tall, but not too short, not a size 10, but not a size 7 either. We were all some shade of brown, with Shaundra being the lightest, Niecee the darkest, and the rest of us looking almost the same color sometimes depending on the light. The only thing that really made me stand out were my hazel eyes, what the boys used to call "cat eyes" in junior high and high school. But at five feet eight inches and almost 190 pounds, Shaundra had a grace and sexiness about her that made the rest of us look like girls. I used to think it was her hair that made her sexy. Like Niecee, she used to wear her hair long, cutting to the middle of her back. After the divorce she went shoulder length and that looked good, too. But on her last birthday, when we all decided to throw her a surprise dinner, she showed up with her hair dyed pitch-black and cut so short, you couldn't even really call it an Afro. And that's when I knew it wasn't the hair.

"Great, ladies. Your walks are looking very stripperesque."

In sets of three, we'd taken turns making rotations around the pole. Once we got the hang of that, Casey switched us to smokeys.

Since Shaundra and I both chose to go second on techniques, we always ended up working our individual pole at the same time.

"Okay," Casey said, "what I want you to do is get arm distance from the pole and bend over toward it, flattening your back."

I moved a small step away from the pole and bent at the waist.

"Okay, put your hands on the pole, and what I want you to do is sway your hips to one side then the other." She looked forward at me then back at Shaundra. "Good. Now I want you to add a little rotation in the hip so that you are going side to side and up and down at the same time."

I looked back at her while she demonstrated. Something about the up and down was catching me up. She walked over to me in her black micro shorts and six-inch platforms and moved my hips through the proper motion a few times before returning to her pole.

"Looking good, ladies. Now that you have that part, point your finger downward on each side of the pole and glide your hands down slowly while letting one knee bend each time you move your hand. Now let your head lower naturally." Casey glanced back at Shaundra. "You whore—you have it perfect already." The girls on the side line giggled and so did Shaundra.

At any other time a woman calling me or any of my girls a whore would have been grounds for letting loose, but I found myself feeling a little jealous. I smoothed my ponytail with both hands and tried to get it right.

"Okay, next group up."

In between working technique on the pole, Shaundra and I both stretched our legs and watched the other two girls execute the movements. By the end of the hour class, we had learned thirteen different moves, and I had been called *"whore"* once. We were so pumped after class, we paid an additional thirty dollars each to take the Body Beautiful class taught by Imani, a full-bodied sistah, who had a completely different approach to healthy female sexuality.

About fifteen minutes after eight, we jumped into Shaun's silver Camry. Shaundra barely got the driver's side door closed before she started talking mess.

"You loved it, didn't you?"

I kept my demeanor reserved. "I wouldn't say *love,* but it was an interesting experience to say the least."

"Kiss my ass." We both started laughing.

"You know your girl. That was amazing."

"I know! Which class did you like better?" She finally started the car.

I sat back and tried to replay both experiences in my head. "I liked Casey, but I really liked Imani too. Girl, I don't know; they were both good."

"I thought so too." She laughed and started singing: "Shaun and Shay droppin' it like it's hot. Whoop, Whoop!"

"I'll tell you what, though," I said, putting on my seat belt, "if we ever do this again, we better pay online to get the discount, 'cause I'm not ever dropping sixty bones like that again."

"I was happy to pay it. The way Brandi and Niecee try to spend my money, it's a wonder I get to do anything for myself."

"Yeah." I thought about what Mark would do if he knew I'd spent sixty dollars on pole class while he was teaching Wednesday night Bible study.

Shaundra flicked her right blinker and waited for the car in front of her to turn. "I was thinking. Maybe once our pole comes we could do this once a month to pick up new moves. We can even invite Brenda and Karina to come along."

I started laughing. "Now you know Karina wouldn't be caught dead up in there. Come on now. And Brenda . . . I think the only reason she agreed to the pole thing in the first place is because Niecee always messes with her about the fact that she can't dance."

"Yeah, I guess this is just a me and you thing." She shot me a look. "Thanks for coming."

"Girl, you're welcome."

After Shaundra dropped me off, I took a quick shower and did something I hadn't done in a long time—I rubbed jasmine-vanilla lotion all over my body, took out a silk camisole and matching black panties, and jumped in bed early to build upon a couple of the techniques I had learned from Imani.

The Body Beautiful class wasn't a masturbation class by any means, but it wasn't a how-to-strip-for-a-man class either. It was a love-your-own-body class. The instructor asked us to grab a mat and find a comfortable spot on the studio floor. As we students laid out our mats, Imani went around the room and lit incense and candles. She said the scent was blackberry-plum. We closed our eyes and she asked us to let the music get under our skin, into our breathing.

I let out a few deep breaths and let my head drop to the side. I almost wanted to cry from how relaxed I felt. She told us to let go of everything outside of the class. There were no mothers-in-law or husbands in this space. There were no children. There were no jobs, deadlines, health issues, or distractions. There was only that moment, our own breath and skin.

After a few moments of breathing and clearing our minds, she asked us to keep our eyes closed and to place both of our hands onto our breasts.

A wave of discomfort shot through my body.

She told us to keep our hands there. That most of us had never really enjoyed the feel of our own skin or the give and sensuality of our own breasts. She asked us to move past the discomfort into the safety of ourselves.

With all my heart I wanted to move my hands away, but I didn't. I followed her instructions and began to massage my breasts. I traced them with the tips of my fingers. I pressed them gently.

From there she asked us to feel our stomachs, and then the inside of our thighs. I raised my right leg into the air and let my fingers send tingling waves through my sweatpants and into my skin. I breathed. By the end of the night, I had felt every part of my body—my face, the bottoms of my feet, my earlobes—every part but one. She said that once we had owned every part of ourselves, including the space between our legs, we would never be exactly the same again. And that was my homework assignment.

I had masturbated before, but never just to the feeling of my own self. Usually as I touched myself, I imagined my fingers were the fingers of Morris Chestnut, Lenny Kravitz, LL, Darius Johnson—anyone but Mark. Our fantasy days had passed years ago.

I lay on freshly laundered sheets in my black camisole. The

silk was cool against my skin. When I felt the moment was right, I slipped my panties off and placed them under my pillow. First I felt the coarse, soft hairs, then I took my middle finger and ran it down the contour of my clitoris. This was my vagina; I had never thought of it that way. I mean, I knew it was mine—technically, it was on my body, but I had never owned it. It had always been relegated to just kinda, you know, *down there*. I wanted to yell "This is my pussy" at the top of my lungs, but I didn't. I merely followed the folds. I rubbed my fingers across the hairs and felt my juices. I stuck my finger in and then pulled it in and out until my clitoris needed the touch of my left hand to make me climax. And after I did, I fell asleep, feeling more complete than I had in a long time.

5

Putting on a pair of six-inch heels and dancing across a stage half-nude couldn't be that difficult, Brenda thought. Getting through the police academy was difficult. Being called giraffe by the boy she was in love with all through junior high and high school was difficult. This had to be easier than any of that. She read the ad again. *Girls, Girls, Girls!!! Take home up to 1,000 bucks a night. New bodies needed. Amateur Contest every Tuesday 9:30 P.M.*

It was Sunday. She sat on the couch with a cup of Kaffree Roma in her lap, her furry, leopard-print slippers perched on the edge of the coffee table. She sipped. She was excited, yet at the same time felt scared out of her mind. Brenda wasn't the greatest dancer, but so what. She had breasts, a firm behind, and a magic patch between her thighs. *Anything else is extra,* she told herself. She stared at the body of the girl in the ad, then settled her attention squarely on the face. The girl looked like a normal white girl—small breasts, brown shoulder-length hair—with her butt poked out. She could have seen her in the grocery store twenty-five times, but just looking at her face, she wouldn't know she was a stripper at Club Nut. She choked a little on her almost coffee and wiped her mouth with the back of her gown's sleeve. What if somebody saw her? Someone she knew, like her judge or somebody who'd appeared in her courtroom for child custody? Someone from high school? Niecee? She would never hear the end of it. She would probably have to sell her momma's old house and find a job in another district. She stared at the ad again. The thought of backing down made her posture droop. She wanted this. She wanted to be stared at on stage. She wanted to feel moist money being placed under the strap of her G-string. She giggled nervously to herself; she didn't even have a G-string. All she had were grandma drawers, and most of them were white or beige. She had to do this. Her mind was already made up, and the sooner she acted, the better. She just needed to figure out how.

6

The first thing that struck me as strange was that Brenda had "Milkshake" playing in the background when I drove up. I'm not saying anything is wrong with that song, but it is definitely not Brenda-type music. She is more of an O'Jays, Commodores, *big* Luther kind of girl. The second thing that was wrong was that Brenda, dear, sweet Brenda, who had been faithful to the press 'n' curl since the first semester of junior high, had a weave. A light brown straight weave, with blondish streaks here and there. I wanted to get the scoop so bad I could barely contain myself. But I waited. I pulled behind Shaundra's Toyota Camry, rolled up the windows of the truck, and walked gingerly across the street with my blanket, black trash bag full of clothes I couldn't fit into anymore, a set of knives, a few VHS movies, and a beaded divider at the bottom of the bag. I gave Brenda a sister-girl hug then commenced to place my blanket to the right of the walkway, just about a foot from the sidewalk.

"Girl, I'm sorry I'm late, how's the yard sale been going?"

She looked at me, then looked back at the four blankets of bric-a-brac, a blanket of piled clothes, and two side tables with an old turntable atop one of them. "Okay. *I guess.*" She smirked a little. "I saved you some space in the front."

"I saw, thanks." Something was definitely different with her. "Did Shaundra tell you we went to a pole dancing class on Wednesday night? Fun. You should have been there."

I looked up a second too late from placing a navy blue sweater on my blanket, but I could almost swear I saw Brenda roll her eyes.

"I *could* have been there had someone called me."

I plopped a couple more sweaters down. "I'm sorry for not calling. We honestly just didn't think it would be your thing. But if we go again, I'll make sure we call you. Okay?"

"Funny, going to a pole class *wouldn't be my thing*, but pitching in almost a hundred fifty dollars for a pole is. I know Niecee thinks I'm a joke, but I'm starting to wonder what you and Shaundra think."

"*Bren-da*," I said, "it was an oversight. It wasn't some 'let's keep Brenda out of the loop' scheme. I didn't even want to go. Shaun had to force me."

"Forget about it." She rolled her eyes again.

I was trying to be patient, but I was in no mood for her little attitude. "Where's Shaundra?" I asked.

"On the toilet, like she's been most of the morning."

"She's sick?"

"If that's what you want to call it. She started fasting on that dieter's tea Karina recommended and it gave her the runs." Brenda tipped her head forward.

"Oh," I said, taking a quick look at her weave. Not that I expected it to look janky or anything, but it had turned out pretty good. I wondered if Niecee's comment a few weeks ago about her hair thinning around the forehead, like she'd been doing braids too long, had pushed her over the edge.

Brenda was seated in one of the three lawn chairs positioned to the west side of the merchandise. She didn't say anything else. Just stared up at me as I straightened out a beaded door divider that Marcus thought made the house look ghetto-fabulous.

"What?" I asked, starting to get irritated, which was a bad sign considering I'd just gotten there.

"Nothing."

I turned and placed the beads on the edge of my blanket, but I could still feel Brenda staring.

"Don't get an ass-whuppin' today, Brenda. It's already been a hard Sunday and Marcus is mad because I haven't been to church three Sundays in a row."

Brenda screwed open the cap of her 7UP, and I waited for her to take a sip. "I should probably just let Shaundra tell you—but, you're gonna find out anyway."

I really think I wanted to sucker punch her in the leg. I crossed my arms.

"She got another one, Shay."

I rolled my eyes and pretended not to know what she was talking about. I pulled a set of cheap knives out of the bag. "Another pole?" I said lackadaisically. I hoped she would just let it go.

She didn't. "From Darius, Shay. She got another one."

I really can't tell you what I pulled from the bag next. The world slowed down for me. I felt my arms moving, brushing against the thick, black plastic, but I completely lost time. I wanted to smile almost as much as I wanted to cry. And if I would have been at home, all by myself, I would have done both.

"You want me to get it? She left it on the table in the kitchen."

I gently dropped the bag to the grass and dusted my hands on my jeans. "I'll get it."

I imagine some walks are always longer than others. The wedding walk. The divorce court walk. The death walk. This was my Darius walk. The one that destabilized my center with each step. The one I made whenever he missed me enough to track me down.

I sat across from the stove at the small, metal-rimmed table that had been positioned in the same spot at the window since I was in eighth grade. I glanced around the kitchen and noticed Brenda's mom's old watermelon cookie jar that I was sure was empty now. I was alone, not because I was by myself, but because there was too much going on inside of me that I couldn't express. I repositioned my chair to face the window so that just in case Shaundra was released from bathroom duty, I wouldn't have to look her in the eye as she passed through the kitchen, at least not immediately anyway.

The envelope was handmade, which told me he was either feeling sentimental or out of money on his books. In small block

letters, in the upper left corner, I read: *Darius William Johnson.*
Then sprawled in lyrical cursive writing with flourishes that
looped and curled was my name: *Mrs. Shay William Johnson.* He
was a liar in the worst kind of way and I hated him. How can you
break every promise you've ever made to someone? A crackhead
had to have better odds.

Shay-shay,
Girl I miss you. You ain't come to see a niggah in a heartbeat.
I'm just sittin here in the barracks thinkin bout you, all lonely
and shit. I talk to that niggah Ben bout you sometimes and
stuff, but I'm knowin, he don't know shit bout having the love
of a good woman in his life. I do. On the real, girl. I still need
you. Can't nobody do me right like you. I just picture your
sweet face and my dick gets hard. I remember what you know
how to do with that mouth of yours, that tongue, them lips.
Fuck, I miss you baby.

Do you ever be thinkin about me? I mean, like what it
would be like to have your man, who ain't had sex in two and
half years, up in you? Ridin you like I'm gonna wear a hole
through your pussy? I'd make it wet, suck it dry and make it
wet again. You a freak, I know you think about me every time
that punk ass niggah touch you. Right Shay?

Anyway, my arms are 22 inches now. I got some guns baby.
I think my dick grew bout an inch too. I'm messin wit cha, but
I know it's harder than the last time it touched your pussy. You
gonna have to get up here. Just get in the car driving north
and come see me. I need to see you. You the only reason I ain't
gone crazy in this joint.

I hope you like the flowers and shit I drew you. Touch it for
me, kay, Shay?

Your one and only niggah,
Darius

The barracks? Fucking disgusting. What, is he supposed to be away in the military or something? *Fuck you, Darius. Mothafucka. And your momma.* I was so angry I didn't know what to do with myself. And then, just when I thought I was going to scream my lungs out, I started to cry. I think it was looking at all the beautiful, detailed flowers he had stenciled around the body of the letter. This is what all of his talent and love for me amounted to. A sheet of paper and a wet dream. I wanted to kill Darius. And at the same time, I wanted to feel his arms around me. Punk-ass.

I sat there, wondering why Marcus never got the same hold on me that Darius had always had, and still did. It didn't make sense.

Mark was different from the boys in my high school classes. He was older, already into a four-year college, and he didn't smoke weed. Weed was a national pastime in my neighborhood. A forty-ounce, weed, and sex—you could count on that almost any night of the week. I wouldn't even have met Mark if it wasn't for Shaundra. The Saturday Darius got picked up on his first weapons trafficking offense, I spent the night at Shaundra's house. Nothing could console me. The only person who really understood how I was feeling was Darius's mom. She cried, I cried, she told me that she was going to put her house up for Darius's bail. That's when I told her, "I would put my soul up for bail if I could." Why did I say that? Shaundra wasn't any more religious than I was, but just hearing me say that into the telephone, she knew I was in too deep. That's how I ended up in church that Sunday morning. Landed right smack in Marcus Gaines's singles Bible study class. I really think it was Shaundra's momma's suggestion, but I don't know the truth about that to this day. Shaundra just said, "We are going to church tomorrow; you can wear something of mine."

Like hell I wanted to go anywhere near anybody's church. If God had listened to me in the first place, Darius wouldn't have been in jail. He was only doing it for us. Trying to make enough money so that we could have a bomb prom, then have something

left over for an apartment deposit. Once we graduated, he was
going to get a real job at UPS or the Postal Service, or become a
cashier at Ralph's. God didn't listen to me, so I sure didn't want to
go to church to listen to his henchmen.

And there was Mark. All dressed up in what looked to be a
well-made suit. His teeth were really straight, his skin was velvet
mocha, and two dimples deepened on either side of his cheeks to
emphasize the major points of his message.

He was teaching out of Hebrews about us having a high priest
who was touched by the pain of our infirmities. "Jesus was
tempted on every side," he said, "and still found blameless.
Therefore we can go to him to find mercy and forgiveness for our
sins."

Whatever. I was bored, I was tired, and the panty hose Shaundra loaned me were making my legs itch. I thought about Darius
having to do a cavity search and sleep in a cell with other men
and only one toilet. It took everything I had not to cry angry, bit-
ter, sorrowful tears. Before I raised my hand, I knew my momma
would have backslapped me in front of Jesus if she heard what I
was about to say.

"Yes, miss, would you please give your name to your fellow students."

"I'm Shay. I want to know how is it that God, *Jesus,* can understand the temptation of our sin if he never sinned? It just don't
make sense to me. I mean, when you sin, you get further and further into it and it takes a lot to get out of it. If you ain't ever
sinned, I mean I kinda get how you can forgive, but I don't really
see how you are entitled to understand it. If you ain't never had a
guy on top of you in the backseat of a car, how you gonna know
how to get out of it?"

"Good question, Sister Shay. Does anyone want to give a shot
at an answer?"

Some big girl in burgundy raised her hand a little too excitedly
for me. I didn't care what the heifer had to say. I wanted to hear

his answer. Mark was patient and kind, I could tell that. He absorbed all of the hostility of my question and smiled at me without the slightest bit of accusation. For a half second, I almost smiled back.

He seemed nice enough. Like a guy who wouldn't end up in jail three weeks before my senior prom. I could kill Darius for listening to his uncle and getting involved in that shit. Things were always going wrong between us. I found myself watching more and more of Mark's movements, listening to the calm in his voice and wondering why I never dated a guy like him. He wouldn't get locked up on me and break my heart.

But I loved Darius, and he was the only guy I had ever been with. Darius and I had sex every time we could catch a moment and six feet of vertical or horizontal space. We had unsanctioned, dirty, jungle-love, give-me-some-mo' sex. And I liked it that way. I had gotten used to doing things behind God's back. That's what every teenager who was raised Pentecostal like I was learned to do. Don't obey the rules unless you have to—bend them, break them, trample them under your feet—and pretend God doesn't notice because you don't talk to him about it.

Once I married Mark, how was I supposed to change that way of thinking? Tell me sex is bad and dirty my entire life, then expect it to change on the day I get married? I don't think so. There should be a debriefing or deprogramming process you go through six months before your wedding day. You can't just click off your beliefs, even if you've tried your best never to follow them. And that's what's wrong with me and Mark. We are still on opposite sides. No matter how many ways I twist it, he works for the Man. The Man-Man. God doesn't like nasty-raunchy. I do.

Pre-preacher, we had some pretty steamy times. I used to love for Mark to strip me down to just my hoop earrings and touch me in places. I loved his dimples, the way his full lips squished against my own, then enveloped all of my bottom lip until I felt a gentle pull. That pull used to drive me crazy. Now I make love to him with my clothes on. It wasn't always this way. It didn't have to be this way.

"Fuck it," I said to myself. Thinking about the past wasn't going to change a damn thing. I dried my tears. Sucked up every last one and got up. Darius was my past—my distant past—and I wasn't going to let myself forget it.

Brenda was still sitting in the same place she had been when I last saw her, Kelis's album still playing in the background. I plopped down.

"Your hair looks cute, Brenda," I said, grabbing a 7UP from the small ice chest.

"Thanks, I figured it was time for a change."

"You bought some new albums too, huh?"

"Yep, you know, it's good to broaden your horizons sometimes. *Big* Luther can't get you through everything."

I chuckled. Brenda was starting to get a sense of humor.

She touched my leg. "Are you all right, Shay?"

Her touch almost made my heart give way. *Suck it up, heffa,* is all I could think to tell myself. "Yeah, you know how stupid Darius's ass is, he just wants me to send some money to put on his books to buy cigarettes and shit. You know how trifling he is; he don't want nothin'. I'm not thinking about Darius. It's his momma who really pisses the hell out of me, though."

I could tell from Brenda's expression that she was about to break out into police officer mode. "I know you don't want to hurt Darius's feelings, but why don't you just tell Shaundra not to take the letters. You don't have to read them, Shay. You don't owe him or his momma anything. You made the decisions you thought were best for your life. What's done is done."

She was referring to the fact that I got married on Darius's birthday. On purpose. It was spiteful, I know, but at the time, I just needed to lash out. Sending the wedding invitation to his momma's house was the twist of the knife.

"I know; it's all over. I'm happily married and he just has to accept that I'm not his anymore."

"That's right. Just let him go." She slapped my leg again.

"Whew, the drama." I feigned a laugh. "You ain't never lied, girl; you ain't never lied! Let me go turn this music up so we can get our groove on." I got up, Darius's letter folded and tucked securely in my back pocket.

7

"Why couldn't you just be my momma? Dang, I can't stand her." Brandi twisted her face and rolled her eyes back into her head.

"I'm too fine to be anybody's momma. Shit, I got too many thangs left to do with this body." Niecee laughed.

"You are too stupid, Aunt Niecee." Brandi slapped Niecee's arm and threw herself on the bed, stomach first.

Niecee leaned her shoulders onto Brandi's back. "Well, don't blame your momma; she ain't never had no taste anyway."

"It's just a wife-beater and a miniskirt, shoot. It's not like I was trying to go to school in lingerie."

"Shhh." Niecee stared toward the door.

"Brandi, don't make me have to tell you again. *GET DRESSED!* You are not wearing that mess to school, so you may as well stop the whining."

Brandi dragged her limp body to a sitting position on the bed. "Auntie Niecee said I could borrow it."

Shaundra could have strangled Niecee. "I don't care what Niecee told you; she's not your momma, I am, and I said *hell no.* Now what?"

Brandi jumped up and forged past Shaundra, careful not to bump into her like she really wanted to do. "You just wanna make me look stupid around my friends. I can't stand you!"

Brandi had almost cleared the danger zone when Shaundra snatched her back by her pajama top. Shaundra spoke calmly. She could feel sweat beads developing on her face. "Don't make me slap the hell out of you, Brandi Lynn." She stared her in the eye. "I am not your friend and I do not care what you can stand. Go get your little ass in there and get dressed. Jeans, pink tennis shoes, and the pink T-shirt with Nike across the front."

Shaundra let go and Brandi pulled away from her. "Momma," Brandi said forcefully, trying not to scream. "My pink tennis shoes are Adidas. I can't wear those with a Nike shirt. I can't mix gear like that; I'm gonna look dumb."

Shaundra crossed her arms over her chest. "You should have thought about that before you tried to smuggle that little ho-ish outfit out of the house. You're gonna get tired of listening to Niecee. Now go put on what I told you to before I make you really look stupid. GO!"

Brandi slammed her bedroom door. Shaundra heard the lock click and turned back toward her sister. Niecee was reclined with one leg on the bed and one leg off.

Shaundra walked up to her; her black silk pajama bottoms touched Niecee's knee. "I'm not gonna keep telling you, Niecee. Stop getting in the middle; you're only making things worse between us. I'm her mother."

"Shaundra," Niecee said from her reclined position, "get the fuck out of my room, please. Thank you."

"This is my house. You don't tell me where to go in my house and you don't tell my daughter she can wear a shirt that says *I go both ways* across the chest to school."

Niecee laughed.

"It's not funny, Niecee. You keep this shit up and you're going to have to go. I can't have you undermining my authority. It's not right."

Niecee placed her arms behind her head. She spoke calmly, "Do you really want to know what wasn't right? Hmmm?" She gave Shaundra a moment to realize what she was about to say. "Mr. Leon wasn't right, Shaundra. But I did it anyway, didn't I?" Niecee stared at her sister and waited for her to say something. It frustrated Niecee that Shaundra never had a reply for this. "Get the fuck out of my room, Shaun. It ain't my fault your daughter can't stand your ass. Look at yourself, not me." Niecee turned over, and with that, the conversation was over.

Shaundra didn't know what else to say. She never knew what to say when Niecee brought up Mr. Leon. Niecee had saved Shaundra from Otis Leon. He had really wanted Shaundra in the first place. Niecee handled it. Shaundra still owed her, and she knew it.

When she walked into Brandi's room, Brandi was dressed in the pink Nike shirt, jeans, and pink Adidas, lying across her twin-sized Chris Brown comforter in tears. Shaundra hated when Brandi's feelings were hurt, but Brandi needed to understand that Shaundra was still in charge—no one else was, especially not Niecee.

Shaundra stepped quietly over to the bed and nudged Brandi to scoot over. "You know, just because you lock the door doesn't mean I don't have the key." She jangled her Betty Boop key chain to the back of Brandi's head.

Brandi jerked, but kept her face close to the wall.

"Brandi, can I talk to you for a moment?"

She shrugged her shoulders.

Shaundra shook her head. "I'm still your mother. You need to answer me, not shrug your shoulders."

Brandi rolled over slowly and covered her eyes with her arm. "What?" she said, muffled under her tears.

Shaundra chose to let it pass; otherwise she was going to strangle Brandi.

"Do you remember how when you were a little girl, you used to come to me when you felt bad or when you were really happy about something?" Just asking the question made emotion well up in Shaundra's chest.

Brandi shrugged her shoulders again. "I guess."

Shaundra breathed deeply. "Well, I want that back, Dee. You used to be my little girl. We used to be friends."

There was a long pause before Brandi spoke. "We were probably never really friends. You're my *mom*. How am I supposed to be friends with the same person who spanks me at *sixteen*? Anyways, *you* just said yourself that you weren't my friend when you were screaming at me a few minutes ago. Aren't you contradicting yourself?"

Shaundra couldn't figure out how Brandi's mouth had gotten so quick and nasty. She knew that Brandi resented the spankings, but sometimes they were the only thing that worked. "I don't know what to say. You want to throw something in my face that's not entirely my fault. If I spank you, it's not because I want to, it's because you need it."

"Well, Auntie Niecee doesn't spank me. She gets me, that's why she is my best friend."

It felt like someone had slammed a hammer into her chest. The hurt made her not want to look at her daughter. "You know, Dee, I'm glad that you and Niecee are becoming friends now that she lives with us again. That's really great; your auntie loves you. I don't think she would ever do anything to intentionally hurt you." Shaundra paused, knowing that she had to tread carefully. "But just remember that your auntie and I have a very complicated relationship. I don't think you need to know everything that happened between us, but sometimes sisters don't always see eye to eye. Sometimes things happen that pull them apart, and it's not one person's fault over the other one's."

Brandi took her arm from her face. "Auntie Niecee already told me why y'all don't get along."

Shaundra almost jumped out of her skin. "What do you mean?"

"*I mean*"—smart-ass was written all across Brandi's face—"I know what happened."

Niecee would have to be the worst kind of person to tell a child something like that. The thought of it made her pissed as hell with Niecee again. "What did she tell you?" Shaundra said, commanding, not asking.

"Why I got to tell you all my secrets? Shoot, you already know the answer."

If the answer was what Shaundra thought it was going to be, she was going to pack up Niecee's shit personally and throw her the fuck out. "Girl, you better answer my question before you get an ass whupping right now."

Brandi socked the air. "Because she stole your boyfriend in high school and 'cause guys always liked her better. I swear, when I turn eighteen I'm moving straight up out of here."

Shaundra got up from the bed. Strangling Brandi was a distant afterthought. All she could think of was the fact that Niecee didn't tell Brandi the truth.

"Brandi, you are walking a fine line between getting kicked out of my house and going to live with your father or having me beat your ass like you are a grown woman. Don't keep testing me, okay? It's going to backfire on you. Apologize."

Brandi kicked the bed. "I didn't do nothing. All I did was tell you the truth, and look how you treat me. I wish Auntie Niecee really was my momma."

Shaundra's arms crossed her chest. "You didn't do anything? Besides lying, do you know what the term *I go both ways* means?"

Brandi starting giggling under her breath, but stopped herself quickly.

"I'm not playing with you, Dee; answer my question."

Brandi wiped her eyes. "It's just a joke, Momma. Dang, it don't mean nothin'."

"Everything means something, Dee. Don't think you're about to do and say any and everything in life and it's not going to catch up with you."

"I'm not saying that." Brandi flailed her arms and turned her head toward the wall again.

"That is exactly what you're saying. *I go both ways?* Have you lost your mind?"

She smacked her lips. "It's not a big deal, Momma, really. Auntie Niecee just said that it would make guys more attracted to me. That they like that type of girl."

So many things crowded Shaundra's mind, but if she said one of them she honestly thought that she might kill Brandi. "Get your books and go eat breakfast while I get dressed so I can take you to school. I'll deal with you and your Auntie Niecee later."

8

By the time our pole came, Shaundra and Niecee were on the outs and Shaundra had pulled Niecee from the pole time-share program.

"When she pays me the hundred and thirty-five dollars she owes me, she can have her week. Fuck a payment plan or a favor."

Shaundra cursing and being mad at Niecee didn't surprise me. Shaundra had a temper of sorts, and the Niecee-Shaundra saga had been going on since junior high school. What caught me off guard was the fact that she refused to talk about the situation. Shaundra always opened up to me, but for some reason she was being distant.

After getting the call that the pole had arrived, Brenda and I showed up within minutes of each other. It wasn't hard to tell something was going on. Just days before, Shaundra had been on an all-tea diet, trying to drop ten pounds, and now she was sitting on the couch with her afghan over her feet with Lay's ranch potato chips and spinach dip in her lap. A glass of chardonnay was on the coffee table, and the uncorked bottle was sitting nearby. The tension in the house was thick, punctuated by no hellos from Niecee or Brandi and slamming doors.

"If you break it, you're going to pay for it," Shaundra yelled back as Brandi closed her door after leaving the bathroom. "I take cash and ass-checks."

I looked at Brenda and she gave me the "you better ask" look. "Girl," I said, "I can't believe the pole is finally here. We should give ourselves a name or something." I adjusted the metal rim of my eyeglasses on my nose. "Maybe the Pole Rotators or something like that."

"What about Chocolate Swirl or the Good Girl Pole Riders. Pretty Polers."

"Umph," Shaundra said, leaning to pour more wine into her glass, but not picking it up.

"Hard day at work, girl?" I asked.

"No."

"Brandi and Niecee?" Brenda asked with a light voice.

"Okay," Shaundra said, putting the foil bag and dip container on the table. She brushed her hands against each other. "Since Niecee is out of the rotation, I figure I can have the pole two weeks and each of you a week a month, or we can split the hundred thirty-five and each get the pole ten days a month."

Her demeanor was businesslike and less than warm. I wasn't sure what I wanted to do. Mark was already getting on me about being too loose with money, so I decided to be sneaky. Brenda was the most penny-pinching person I knew, so I figured I'd put it in her hands. "Well, that would be what?" I calculated quickly in my head. "Forty-five dollars apiece. Brenda?"

"Whatever, I'll pay it," she said.

"Shay, you take it the first ten days, Brenda, you're next, and I'll be last."

I hadn't expected to get the first rotation, but I was psyched. "That's cool with me. I will put the pole to good use."

Brenda smirked her thin little lips. "Well, if it is all right with the two of you, I would like to go first."

Shaundra looked at me. Brenda was really on one as far as I was concerned; she was officially on my last nerve. "Well," I said, "I think I'd rather stay with the arrangement Shaun proposed. Unless there is some reason I shouldn't?"

I looked at Brenda. "You can just drop it off on my porch when you are done." She got up from the love seat. "See you later, Shaundra. I hope you feel better."

"Thanks, girl. I will." They hugged, and Brenda walked to the door. I didn't care that Brenda was leaving me out of the hug loop, but if felt strange. Shaundra had even commented herself that Brenda had been acting out lately. My throat felt dry and my feelings were a little hurt. "Is that it?" I pointed to a silver case that was about four feet long.

"Yep." Shaundra let out a sigh. "All right, I'm going to sleep. I will talk to you later. Give me love." Shaun came over to me and I stood up. The hug was friendly-professional. That was the first time Shaundra had ever kicked me out of her house.

I walked to my truck by myself, holding the pole case in front of me with both hands. It was heavy, so I walked fast and locked my arms out so they wouldn't get too tired. Funny enough, my arms were still the slightest bit sore from the pole class Shaundra and I had taken together. We'd had so much fun, and now I was left feeling disappointed. The day our pole came was supposed to be an exciting day of liberation and togetherness. Instead, it felt like a journey I was about to start all by myself. I clicked my alarm and slid the shiny silver case onto the backseat. "You're trippin', Shay," I told myself. "You and your girls are tighter than ever. This is just one of those funky days where everyone's attitude seems a little premenstrual." I said this, but inside, I wasn't sure.

9

Brenda was still mad at Shay, but she wasn't going to waste her time dwelling on it. Shay always got what she wanted; that's the way things had been forever.

She sat in the strip club parking lot, thinking about the fact that she was at the bottom of the barrel as far as her friends were concerned. Even Niecee, who wasn't even a bona fide member of the crew, had more pull than she did. She wondered if her lack of status was because she lacked range. Even the car she drove was old; it had been old when she got it, but it worked, and rarely did she get rid of anything until it lost its usefulness. She washed out Ziploc bags until they got holes in them. She got good leather shoes reheeled and kept her mother's old sewing machine handy to repair rips and tears, even in socks. She didn't count herself frugal, just a good steward of her resources. She was the only one of any of her friends who had any serious savings in the bank, except for Shay, and anything Shay had was only because of Marcus. Her practical sensibility had always been a source of pride, but now she felt dependable and boring.

Brenda thought back to when they were kids and they used to play truth or dare together. Out of the four of them, everyone else would mix it up, picking dare at least part of the time. In six years, Brenda never chose dare once. Even when they begged her and offered to buy her a Bomb Pop or give up their favorite T-shirt. As much as she wanted to sometimes, she just couldn't do it. Dare wasn't in her fiber.

Brenda glanced up at the club and then back to her hands. She didn't know what she was so afraid of. The club didn't look like anything that impressive or intimidating to her from the outside. It was steel gray with dark blue moldings around the main entrance. Brenda had showed up early and had been sitting in her 1990 Infiniti Q-45 watching people come in and out for over an hour. She wanted to get a feel for the world she so desperately wanted to enter into. It was a *gentleman's* club, so it made sense to her that most of the patrons were men. She'd always gotten the idea that men flocked to these kinds of places in packs. She was amazed by how many men arrived solo. Normal-looking men. Younger. Older. Men who had nice cars and probably had nice wives and children at home. Brenda wondered what made them come here. She wondered if it was the same thing that forced her to come—the desire to feel desired.

Before the wannabe strippers started to arrive for amateur night, it was really easy to see who the real strippers were. They looked like the same women who worked at Denny's or the bank, arriving in their Ford Escorts and the occasional Accord. They wore sweats, little or no makeup, with medium to large duffle bags draped over their shoulders. Brenda started to understand more fully the concept of *working girl* as she sat there watching. Some of these women were indeed girls; they looked like they belonged in a PE class somewhere. Others were clearly women. They had bills to take care of just like she did. She noticed dutiful determination in their strides, not joyful expectation.

Three women in a VW Rabbit pulled into the empty parking space next to her. Brenda glanced over at them, then pretended to look for a pen or something on the passenger side of her car. She felt embarrassed, but she didn't know exactly why. They were all women. They were all going to the same place, but something about them seeing her sitting in the car by herself made her feel dirty and amateurish. As they parked, Moby, rock with a little ghetto-ese, blasted from their speakers. The blonde driver turned off the ignition, and the music was quickly replaced by a rambunctious freedom that Brenda determined only white girls truly had. The two girls in the front howled. Brenda grabbed an In and

Out ketchup packet from under the seat and turned to face the steering wheel. She was sure they were already drunk. The passenger in the back still had her hands waving above her head like the best part of her favorite groove was still playing in her head.

"Bitch, give me my brush," the front passenger said, reaching her open palm toward the backseat.

"I'm not your bitch, bitch," the back passenger said, handing the brush forward. They all burst out laughing.

"Let's get this party crunk!" said the driver. "Whooo!" They all screamed in unison. The driver pushed her door open, and before Brenda knew it, she felt a thud.

"Fuckin' A," the driver said, then jumped out of the car checking for damage to her own vehicle first. She looked at Brenda. "I'm sorry for hitting your car door, but there's no damage, really. Do you wanna get out and check?"

Brenda was at a loss for words. Normally she would have gotten out and inspected thoroughly, even flashed her badge as a slight intimidation tactic. She would have even taken a picture with the spare camera she kept with her jumper cables and Fix-A-Flat in the trunk. Her body was frozen. "Don't worry about it. This car is on its last legs anyway."

"Cool, girl," the driver said, and rustled her hands in the fringe of her miniskirt. "Well, when you come inside, I gotcha on a couple of shots."

"Thanks."

It was almost 9:30, and it was at this point that Brenda knew she didn't have the balls to go in. All of those girls had been dressed so cute. Brenda just hadn't thought out her costume and theme well enough. She would have been going in cold, and making an ass out of herself or being laughed at would have killed her. She looked at herself in the rearview mirror and breathed hard. "This was a bad idea," she said, looking away from the mirror. It was impossible for her to look herself in the eye.

10

I dreamt about him:

I'm in the produce department in the supermarket. I'm perusing the furthest aisle where the apples, oranges, pears, and lemons are stacked. The sign above the oranges says *Sweet California Navel Oranges*. I haven't bought oranges in a while, I think. Mark will eat them even if I don't. I can make orange juice out of them if they start to go bad.

I grab a large paper bag instead of plastic. I start to place the ripest, most colorful ones into the bottom of the bag. I must have three or four pounds when the bag starts to give way. The oranges roll across the white, speckled tile. One gets wedged at the bottom of the bin. Just as I'm about to drop to my knees, a young man who was picking bananas for himself looks in my direction. He comes over, drops to one knee, and starts to pick up all of the strays. I kneel and grab the one under the bin. We make eye contact. He doesn't look away. Instead he looks down at my lips. I'm not sure, but I think his lips are nearing mine. He smiles. His teeth seem lickable. I swear I smell Close-Up toothpaste. He doesn't kiss me. Instead he takes the orange out of my hand and places my hand in his. I feel a slight tug in my shoulder socket. He leads me through two large rectangular doors, through the employee lounge, into the restroom. He locks the door.

I don't even know his name. I know he is *fine*. Six feet two. Bronze. His hands are large and a little rough, like he works with them. The first kiss is light. I like that he doesn't need to ask permission. He just knows that he can. I pretend to fight the slightest bit. He plunges into my mouth harder, but keeps his tongue flaccid enough to cause pleasure. Just as I am adjusting to the aggressiveness of his kiss, he places his hand under the lip of my T-shirt and over one of my lace-covered breasts. He presses, then squeezes. I gasp. He takes his lips to the outside of my shirt and opens his mouth over the other breast, mouthing it from the outside in. My head falls onto his shoulder, and I find myself groping his back. My fingers absorb the heat from his skin. My breasts are engorged, my nipples stubborn and reddened.

"I don't even know you," I say, in a decibel that is barely audible.

He looks up and stings me with his eyes. They are more hazel than brown. "You do know me," he says. "We speak the same heat. If we meet in another life, I will be as familiar."

Bullshit, I think, but it sounds good. He runs his tongue down my stomach and scorches my skin. I brace his shoulders. He is going for the drawstring knotted in my sweats. A part of me is hoping that he's not able to get the knot out. I don't have a condom. He can't be more than twenty-three years old, but I swear, it feels like he knows me. He lowers to his knees. I say no and start to fight him, almost for real. He blocks my jab at his face. The drawstring gives way. Purple lace panties are no defense. As he holds both of my coiled fists in either hand, with his teeth he slides my underwear from over my crotch. I feel air rushing to the area, then his tongue makes its way through thick hairs to my clit. I gasp again when he starts to suck.

"Let it out," he says. "Don't suffocate ecstasy."

I am determined to hold it in. This is too much.

The heel of his shoe clanks against the porcelain toilet with each push of his tongue into me. His hold loosens from my wrists. I take both of my hands and grope the woolliness of his hair. A guttural moan opens up in my throat.

"Ride my tongue, baby. Ride it, Shay."

Shay? How does this man know my name?

Mid-gyration, I bunch his hair in my hands and pull his neck back, away from my snatch. He is no longer bronze, he is pecan brown, almost black. His features are no longer sleek, but full and round.

"Ride that tongue, Shay. Tame that mothafucka." He squeezes my ass cheeks so that his tongue is lodged deeper inside me.

"Give me that pussy, girl." His words are mumbled; his voice sounds almost angry. "If you don't ride it, I'ma spank that ass."

I know this voice. I know the aggressive plays. "*Darius?*"

"Who the fuck would it be?" he says while still licking me. I don't hear his words as much as I feel them ring through my body.

I really start to fight him. "No, Darius. I belong to Mark now."

"Mark's a bitch. This is my pussy."

I am repulsed by him, yet at the same time, I can feel my juices flowing more heavily.

"Darius, stop. I can't take this. It isn't right, baby. Don't do this." I notice the tiled floor has changed from speckled to cement. The toilet is still in its place, but as he pulls me to the ground, my head almost hits the green frame of his bottom bunk.

"Give me this snatch before that niggah Ben comes back, or you gonna have to cum for the both of us."

I slap him. He smiles so that I see the white of his teeth. Darius grabs my arms over my head and pins me to the cement.

"Hit me now," he says.

I try to move my wrists, but I can't break contact with the ground.

"I hate you," I say.

Darius pushes my face away so that my temple hits the cement hard enough to leave a bruise. With my jugular fully exposed, his jaws clamp down on my neck. I don't move. I am prey now. His body spreads over mine. His smell is sweet and pungent; it takes over my breathing space. The heat and moisture are so strong I feel hot and cold at the same time. He is inside me now.

"I told you this was mine. Look how easily I fit."

He doesn't fit as easily as he thinks. It feels like his penis has grown from the last time we did this. Twelve years is too much time, I think. I don't want to want him. I try not to give in completely, but it is too late.

"Shoshannah, unlock the door. *Shoshannah.*"

I opened my eyes slowly. I felt dizzy, like someone had just beat me with a bag of bricks. "Shit," I said under my breath, when I looked out from the center of our California king-size bed and realized that Marcus was home and I still needed to dismantle the pole. I grabbed my glasses from the nightstand and scrambled out of bed trying not to make any noise. This had been my first time working with the pole since I got it from Shaundra, and I hoped the directions hadn't lied when they said it only took thirty seconds to dismantle. I held on to the pole, unscrewed it from a locked position, and pushed the support base out of place with my foot.

"Shoshannah, are you okay?" Mark's voice was starting to sound frazzled.

I began separating the two main pieces. "I'm just waking up. One second, I have a cramp in my leg." I hated to lie to him, but I definitely didn't want him finding out about the pole like this. I unscrewed the ceiling plate from the top of the pole and started putting everything piece by piece in the case.

I saw the crescent-shaped brass knob shake. "I'm almost up, honey, I'll be right there. How has your day been today?"

He didn't respond. I latched the case and pushed it under the bed.

"Hey," I said to Marcus as I unlocked the door. I gave him a hug around the waist.

"Nap?"

"Yeah," I said, pulling away from him. I wondered if he could smell the sex on me. My body was still moist from the intensity; my panties were soaked. "I was really tired today. I finished your laundry, though. I still have to go pick up your beige and both black suits from the cleaners; I'll do it before five. This cramp is really kicking my butt, though."

"Thanks, baby, and I'd appreciate you picking up the suits. I'm going to take all of that for the conference this Thursday. Right or left?"

"Right or left what?"

"Where do you have the cramp?" At six-one, in a dark gray power suit and burgundy tie, his look was intimidating.

"Oh. My right leg. The calf." I limped slowly back to the bed.

"Hey." Mark braced my shoulder. I turned toward him. "Are you feeling all right, Shannah? Let me massage it for you."

"I'm okay, I'll just walk it off." I didn't want Marcus to touch me. I had just experienced the most intense wet dream I'd ever had, and my body ached like Darius had really been inside of me. It was hard to believe it wasn't real.

Mark reached up and smoothed back the wildness of my still unbraided hair. "Is that it?" He looked me in the eyes. "Is anything else bothering you? Are you feeling safe?"

"What are you talking about? We live in Regal Crest. Nothing happens here."

He pulled me to his chest. The faintest scent of Burberry filled my nostrils. "I mean, it's the middle of the day, Shannah, and you have yourself locked in our bedroom. Are you feeling safe emotionally?"

I always locked the door when I needed private time, just in case Mark popped home early from his aerospace nine-to-five. "I'm fine, Mark. I just locked the door. No biggie." I glanced down at the bottom of the bed to make sure the pole case wasn't visible. Mark could spot anything that seemed out of place. He even noticed if I placed the knife handles in the wrong direction in the wooden block.

"Can we talk?" he asked.

I shrugged my shoulders. Peach fuzz from my robe brushed my ears.

Mark faced me at an angle. "Are you still mad about the job thing, Shannah?"

I wasn't going to talk about it again; he had already made his decision. "It was just something Shaundra had mentioned to me. It's not a big deal."

"If it wasn't a big deal, then why did you bring it up, Shannah? I even saw the applications in your folder in the den."

"Don't do that, Marcus. You know I hate when you go through my things. I don't go through your things."

He touched my shoulder, again. "Baby, be glad you have a husband who cares about what's going on in your life. I only want to be involved. That's it. And you already know, you can go through my things whenever you like. What's mine is yours. No secrets."

I hated when he did that, and I knew he knew it. I tightened the belt on my robe, looked him straight in the eye, and tried to keep the calm in my voice. "I'm not you, Marcus. And in terms of the job thing, you already made it clear. You don't want your wife working an hourly job. What else is there to say?" I didn't give him a chance for a rebuttal. I headed for my closet, forgetting to limp.

He employed his "here we go again" voice. "Shoshannah, where are you going?"

I didn't even look back at him. I grabbed a T-shirt, then a fresh pair of sweats from the built-in pullout drawers in the walk-in closet area. I untied my belt and let my robe fall to the carpet. "I just wish you would respect my privacy, Marcus. I wish I could take a job I want to take and not have to worry about how it looks. But forget it. I'm going to go finish my *helpmate* duties and pick up your laundry so then I can get back and make sure your dinner is on the table on time. Pot roast, right? That's what you wanted, with red potatoes, creamed carrots, and corn bread? I better get moving." As I pulled my T-shirt down over my braless breasts, I glanced at his reflection in the mirrored closet door. He was sitting on the edge of the bed with his legs gapped wide, his hands and head hanging between them.

"I don't get you sometimes, Shay. I give you everything. Any other woman who grew up in the hood would wish she had it this good. You have a brand-new house, a good husband. You don't want for anything and you're still not satisfied."

Any other woman from the hood? I whipped around with my sweats in my hand. "Oh, so now I'm *Shay* from the ghetto. The one you singlehandedly saved from a life of welfare and food stamps. I'm Shay when I'm not acting like the perfect wife, right? And you want me to have kids now? So I can be a slave to a whole house full of mothafuckas who are never satisfied with anything I do?" My sweats dropped to the floor. I placed both hands over my mouth. I hadn't meant to say it like that.

Mark rose up. "No, you're Shay when you go off cursing at your husband and your hood rat tendencies resurface. I'll pick up my own laundry. Do what you want for dinner; I'll catch something while I'm out."

"Whatever. You have a purpose for your life, Mark; what about me? I can't fart without you having an opinion about it. Keeping house, cooking dinner, and picking up laundry is not a life."

He didn't slam the bedroom door; he closed it gently, which concerned me more. Maybe if he'd just scream every once in a while, we'd actually get somewhere. I didn't know what to do. I pulled on my sweats, grabbed a sweatshirt, and headed out.

11

Brenda had a few things to rethink. She didn't take the other night in the parking lot as a total defeat; she just needed a new plan. She also needed a different kind of club. A black club, she thought. There, an exotic woman would be appreciated. Brenda glanced through the *Weekly* again. Out of all the clubs in the back of the paper, she didn't see one that pictured all black models. It occurred to her that she might have to do a phone book search by neighborhood. The Workman District would surely have a black club. She'd worked that beat her first two years on the police force. She hated it. But she did remember a couple of hole-in-the-wall places she could look into.

First things first. She needed to find a real costume. Something sexy and elegant that concealed her identity. Brenda jumped up off the couch and made her way to the bedroom. Across from the modest full-sized bed with a white metal frame was her computer desk. She sat in the gray rolling chair and started her internet search. As she entered Google's URL, keywords popped to mind: Rio, Carnival, costume rentals, makeup kits, Mardi Gras. *Mardi Gras.*

Brenda had never been the greatest typist. She punched the keys one by one with both of her index fingers. Several Mardi Gras supply companies came up. In true frugal fashion, she chose the discount option. Small pictures of table decorations, beads, banners, hats, and masks appeared. She didn't know why she hadn't thought of that before. She clicked the icon. "Jackpot," she said to herself. Dozens of multicolored masks appeared. Masks on sticks, masks with plastic bands, feathered masks, plaster and papier-mâché ones. She thought for a minute. Feathers were definitely her thing. One mask at a time, she looked through the entire inventory. There was so much to choose from. After an hour, she narrowed her final selection to two—an all white half-face eagle mask with gold sequins around the eyes and a multicolored mask with blue sequins around the eyes and stray feathers that formed a haphazard tiara effect above the head.

As she created an account password and entered her credit card information, she thought about the fact that she had chickened out the other night. She wasn't proud of it, but she would have to learn to be more patient with herself. She would have never admitted it to anyone, but she had always been a little bit of a nerd. The slower one of the crew. Not the smartest one necessarily, just the one who worked the hardest. She thought about it. She'd never even had a real date all through high school. Even Karina had dated, and Karina was chunky, Brenda thought.

She couldn't finger it, but there was always something about her that made her different. Maybe it was a coolness and a comfort level she never felt with herself. She was pretty enough. At least she thought so. She didn't have Shay's eyes, or Niecee's body, or Shaundra's confidence, or Karina's face and skin, but she had something.

"Anyway," Brenda said, letting go of her past failures and insecurities. She was transforming little by little, and she wasn't going to let fear stop her. She got up from the computer to go look at herself in the bathroom mirror. The hair, she thought staring at her reflection, made the biggest difference of all in her new look. Had she known that all she needed was a twenty-inch honey blond weave with highlights, she would have gotten it done a long time ago. The part down the middle of her head made her feel even more sexy. The stray hairs that fell in her face when she accomplished everyday chores made her feel even more mysterious. The mask would be the capper. All she needed now was for Shay to bring her the pole.

12

Mark not being home wasn't going to stop me from making dinner. Pot roast, red potatoes, carrots, and corn bread were going to be on the table at 7:30 whether he liked it or not. Whether he ate it or not. It was almost 7 P.M. Normally Mark would have been fresh from the shower, making notes for some lesson or sermon at the dining room table as he waited for dinner. I promised myself that I wasn't going to cry. I'd been crying far too much lately anyway. Instead, I kept fixing dinner. I spread real butter over the golden round belly of corn bread cooling on the stove. I ladled the juices from the roast over the potatoes and carrots, then placed the black and white speckled enamel dish back in the oven. Fifteen more minutes was all it needed.

As much as I wanted to be sure, I didn't know if Mark would be home for dinner or not. He usually never missed dinner, even if he had a large lunch at work. Even if I cooked something he didn't want to eat that day. But I think the dig about the children hit him low. He wanted kids. He wanted three or four of them. I wanted them too . . . most of the time. The rest of the time, I wasn't sure I wanted any at all. And sometimes, as awful as it sounds, I wasn't sure I wanted his.

"You have problems, Shay," I said to myself.

As worthless as Darius was, sometimes I still fell back into high school la-la land. We were supposed to have two kids—a boy and a girl. We were supposed to get an apartment and make a decent living together. The sick thing about first love is that it can be the worst thing for you, and at the same time, the only thing you ever really wanted.

Marcus was safe. And to say I didn't love him would be a lie. I loved him the way hurt people love other people. It's almost like I had a glove over my heart. The way I see it, first love is pure and everything else is a reasoning process to figure out safety. Marcus was better than Darius in every way that counted, besides the heart. I could tell that he wasn't going to hurt me in the ways Darius would continue to if I let him. So when Marcus tried to spit game after church, I listened. He was kinda smooth in the way he did it, too. He didn't just invite me to Marie Callender's following the service, he invited Shaundra as well. Shaundra had been attending his young adult Bible class on and off for nine months or so at that point.

At first, I didn't even know it was me Mark was interested in. I figured he was just trying to get in my pants because of the make-out comments I'd made during his Sunday school class. Religious pervs want loving, too. Before we left for the restaurant, Shaundra pulled me aside in the women's bathroom.

"He likes you, girl," she said, grabbing my hand and pulling me into her.

I automatically frowned. "What are you talking about, Shaun? What could he possibly like? That he thinks I'm a ho?"

"Shhh," Shaundra said and pulled me into a stall with her. "Mark's not like that, Shay. I've been in his class for half of forever and he don't ever be trying to pick up girls. He's a cool guy, way better than Darius anyway."

Shaundra was really about to piss me off. "I thought *Darius* was your boy. Now you just turning on him 'cause his luck ran out?" I shook my head. "That's doggish, Shaun."

Shaundra rolled her eyes. "I'm not thinking about Darius's stupid butt. He *is* my boy, and you know my momma and his momma are third cousins." Shaun grabbed my shoulder, and even to this day, I remember the look in her eye. "Darius is seventeen years old; he's already going to youth authority. What do you think is next? Shit." She lowered her voice. "We both know what's next, Shay. You don't want no jailbird, girl. Think about my momma, following that niggah from state to state. You're just getting your heart ready for more tape. He's gonna break it to death, girl."

She wasn't lying. I knew that. Her words still hurt, though. She looked at me like she wanted me to make some decision right on the spot. "So what? You telling me to leave him? I'm just supposed to walk away when he's at his lowest?"

Shaundra realized my heartbreak was still too new. She hugged me and she hugged me tight. Her words fell softly into my ear. "I ain't tellin' you to leave him. I'm just saying look at your choices. If Mark was into me, I would jump on that. Let's just go to lunch and you can see if you dig him at all."

"Hey," Mark said, dropping his keys onto the cherry-stained kitchen counter.

"Hey yourself," I said softly, checking the small battery-operated clock above the sink.

Mark came up behind me, hugged me with one arm, then presented purple orchids to me with the other.

I turned off the water, then wiped my hands on the dish towel. "Thanks," I said, taking the bouquet from his hand and laying it gently on the counter. "I need to put these in a vase."

Mark turned me around to face him. "I'm sorry for everything I said, Shannah."

Just hearing him call me Shannah again hurt my feelings. "You called me a hood rat, Mark." I looked him in the eye and had to turn away because my eyes were starting to water.

"Shannah, I didn't call you a hood rat, but I still shouldn't have said what I said." He squeezed the outside of my arms. Pot roast scents flavored the air. I reached over to turn off the stove. He'd gotten home at 7:35 exactly.

"What's the difference between 'hood rat' and 'hood rat tendencies,' Mark? You married a girl from the hood. If you wanted some Ivy League chick, you should have waited for one. But that's not who I am, and I'm never going to be it."

He kissed my lips and gently pulled my lower lip between his.

"Don't do that," I said, turning away from him again.

"I love you, Shay, Shannah, Shoshannah, just the way you are. I don't want anybody else. You captured me."

I wanted to believe Mark so badly. "Then if you love me, Mark, and you accept me, what's the difference between me having an hourly job or an eighty-thousand-dollar-a-year job besides money? What happens when you leave your Northrop job? What if the money from the church doesn't kick in like you expect it to?"

Mark crouched toward me so that we were eye level. "All eyes are on us now, Shannah. I am one of the youngest men to ever get my own church. If you're working in customer service at Big Lots, how does that look? Like I can't support my wife. Like all the offerings at church need to go to us so my wife won't have to work a six-seventy-five-an-hour job. You have to be sensible. Perceptions count whether we like it or not."

"It's not six seventy-five and I don't care how things *look* anymore, Mark. I'm sick of being in the house. A part of me thinks we should have kids whether we are ready to or not just so that I can have something to do with myself."

"What about your purpose to take care of me so that I can take care of God's work? That's not good enough?"

It wasn't good enough. I leaned against the sink. "Let's just drop it. . . . We're not going to get anywhere with this."

"Don't give up on me, Shannah."

"I'm just tired right now, Mark. Dinner's ready. Are you hungry?"

Mark grabbed my arms again. "What about school? What if you went back to school to get your A.A. or bachelor's?"

"That was eighteen to twenty-two, Mark. I'm thirty. I'm gonna have kids soon, then what, I drop out again?"

"You said you wanted to write a novel. What about that?"

I couldn't help laughing. "I don't know the first thing about writing a novel. Let's eat." I moved away from him and opened the cabinet where the plates were.

Mark leaned against the cutting island. "Shannah, you read all those girl books. You're telling me you couldn't write something better than that?"

I searched his face to see if he was serious. Something in his words had caught my attention. I felt a belief. I wondered if he was just trying to make me feel better and save himself from public embarrassment. "What are you trying to say?"

He came toward me again. "I'm saying find something you want to do that is going to fulfill you. I full-heartedly support that."

"Are you serious?"

"Cross my heart."

"You think I could be an author?" I studied him.

"If that's what you want to do, yes. Maybe you could start a Christian series or something. Think about it as your ministry."

I just stared at Mark for the longest time. "You amaze me, Mr. Gaines," I said, then kissed him on the lips. I paused. "I'm sorry about the kids-slave comment. I'm glad to be your wife."

"How glad are you?" he said, lowering my hand to right below his belt.

I smiled, even though I felt a slight queasiness on the inside. "You trying to start something?"

"Umm-hmm." He guided my hand in a circular motion.

I pulled away from the counter. Mark led me to our bedroom.

After dimming the lights, he sat on the edge of the bed and worked his long fingers to get the knot out of my sweats. He lowered them so that my pubic hair showed above the waistband. As he grabbed me on both side of my hips, I felt a rush through my body. I hadn't felt that in a long time. He began to lick my abdomen; his mouth enveloped my entire pelvic bone on the right side of my body. I let out a low gasp.

"Take off your shirt, Shannah. I want to see you." His request tightened my stomach. I wanted to keep my shirt on; I felt safest with my shirt on, and I didn't have a bra underneath. I slid my arms out of the sleeves and pulled the sweatshirt over my head.

Marcus stopped kissing my stomach momentarily and looked up. "You look beautiful, Shannah."

"Thank you," I said, placing both hands on his head and starting to massage. I felt vulnerable. Mark reached his left hand up toward my breast. I shook. I wondered if Mark could tell the difference between shock and pleasure.

"Are you okay?" he asked.

"Umm-hmm." I nodded, still rubbing his head. I wondered if I had ever felt this awkward about Darius touching me. I wondered if I had ever flinched in the middle of our lovemaking.

Marcus removed my hands from his head and lowered me by the waist to my knees. He never asked me for oral sex; he always positioned me. As I widened my stance on my knees to get a better height, Mark removed the belt from his pants and then unzipped them.

"Try not to get any on my pants, Shannah," he whispered as he pulled my head forward.

I licked my lips and placed his hardening penis into my mouth. As I sucked in and out and his dick got harder, my nose picked up on his pheromones. I started thinking of Darius. Something about the smell brought me back to his letter and the animalistic way he had taken me in my afternoon dream. I felt a flash of wetness build in my vagina. I placed both hands around Marcus's dick, one at the base and one at the tip, and I sucked in stronger, longer strokes. I licked it and took it all into my mouth. And as he grabbed my hair and prepared to come in my mouth, I imagined Darius's fingertips on the back of my head.

The next morning I felt guilty, but extraordinarily horny. Marcus had already left for work by the time I had woken up. Last night had been nice, a better connection than we had had in a long time, but I wondered if it was just because of Darius. The mere thought of him made my juices start flowing. I hated that, that he still had that kind of power over me, but a part of me was grateful. I felt alive when I thought about him. I felt sexual and seductive.

I crawled to the bottom of the bed and looked under the bed ruffle. It was still there. I couldn't wait to pull it out. Just touching the pole and swinging around it made me feel delicious.

I put on a white sports bra and a pair of black biker shorts I hadn't worn in over four years. I looked at myself in the closet door mirror. I was a good size, I thought, but I definitely wasn't as toned as I used to be. My mocha skin puckered into two little rolls above the waistband. Under the waistband, visible whenever I wasn't sucking in my stomach, was a rise about the size of a Nerf ball. My breasts seemed bigger, but longer, and when I turned around, my butt was definitely wider and flatter, and my hair was afro-kinky. I could have stood there, wondering how and when all of this had happened, but I didn't. I wanted to feel empowered, not depressed. I tightened my pink scarf around my head, made a mental note to call my braid girl before the end of the day, and started my workout.

Assembling the pole took me a little less than ten minutes. I pulled on it a few times to make sure it was secure. It turns out Shaundra had ordered a super pole, with rotating possibilities, but there was no way I was ready for that yet. Since the master suite of our house was large, I had about a five-foot radius around the pole as I worked. I closed all of the shades, except for the ones on the French doors that opened to the backyard deck. Since I didn't have any come-fuck-me pumps, as the clear platform stilettos were affectionately called, I put on a pair of black two-inch heels I usually wore whenever I went to church.

I started my walk, a slow and sexy drag around the pole. I reminded myself to cross my feet across my body and to pop my hips. After a few minutes, I started to get a feel for it. "You whore," I said to myself, and started to laugh.

Next I practiced smokeys and frogs. As I built up a sweat, I wondered what Mark would do if he came home one day and saw me dancing on a pole. The idea sent a shiver up my spine, but I didn't let it stop me. I repeated a move my instructor had called the *ballerina* around the pole a few times. Maybe Shaundra was right. Maybe Mark would appreciate a little more spice in his sex life. I definitely needed it, even if he didn't. Sucking his penis, having intercourse, falling asleep, and then occasionally cunnilingus, were pretty tired after twelve years. As I worked on the technical aspects of my movements—making sure my toes were pointed, my back was straight, and that I kept one hip popped at all times—I started to understand how a girl could get caught up in doing this for a living. I felt powerful, and I didn't even have an audience fawning over me. This was my moment.

"Wrap it up," I told myself after glancing at the clock. It was almost 11:30, and I got the strangest feeling that Mark would be coming home again for lunch. Before changing into my usual, sweatpants and a matching sweatshirt, I disassembled my pole.

If he came home, I knew he would be checking for progress, so by twelve o'clock I had planted myself in front of the computer. Dancing on the pole felt like an escape, but sitting at the computer in an attempt to start a book was nerve-racking. In general, the computer area was Mark's. He'd compose most of his sermons at the dining room table, then come to the den, where the large oak desk took up almost as much room as the leather sectional. On one of the far corners of the desk was a picture of Mark and me from our honeymoon cruise, along with a pen set, a ruler, and two packs of Doublemint gum, one opened, one closed. I felt alone and the house felt entirely too quiet.

I reached under the desk to turn the computer on. The vibration of the hard drive starting up buzzed against my leg. I was about to start my first novel, and I didn't know what I was going to say. A part of me felt alive, yet another part of me wondered if Mark was really serious when he made his suggestion. He didn't even read novels; everything in his library was Christian, self-help, or finance related unless it was a novel he had been assigned as coursework in college. When I weighed my options, going to school, having a baby, or writing a book were the only things I felt I could do, and I wasn't really sure I could do any of them. What had I been doing for the last twelve years of my life? It felt like I hadn't done anything important since graduating from high school. Okay, I had married Mark and he was successful in his ministry and in business, but how much of that success could I honestly claim for myself? I cooked all of his meals, watered the lawn and plants, washed his drawers and made sure his shirts were pressed, but what else did I really do besides housemake and hang with my girls whenever Mark's radar wasn't too tight on my ass?

I should have been happy, I knew that, but I wasn't one thousand percent sure I had picked the right life. I wasn't kidding myself; I was aware of the alternatives. Even as I looked back on my high school class, it seemed like many of my former classmates were cracked-out, on some type of government aid, or dead. With those statistics, my life didn't seem like a bad choice. But then, after being bored out of my mind and watching more *Jerry Springer* and home improvement shows than I could bear, I sometimes thought of the ghetto lifestyle with a fond observance. Shaundra would laugh me out of the water when I would talk like this, but so what. Three kids, a paycheck, some food stamps, and conjugal visits with Darius in prison might have suited me just fine.

I clicked the keyboard. "You are stupid, Shay," I said to myself. How did my standards get to be so low? None of my girlfriends were doing that bad financially, and ironically, in one way or another, they all thought of me as lucky. I thought of myself as trapped.

Maybe that's what I should write about, I thought to myself. A pastor's wife who feels trapped, hates going to church, drinks, masturbates too much, and curses like a marine whenever her husband isn't around. I laughed, knowing that Marcus would probably shoot me for doing something like that. I didn't want him to become the laughing stock of his church. I wanted to please him, but I knew off the bat that a Christian novel wasn't in my blood. Deep inside, I already knew what I wanted to do, and it wasn't going to please Marcus at all.

13

Shay left the pole on Brenda's front porch as she had asked. She placed it on its side so that most of the case was hidden behind Brenda's mother's old rocking chair. Brenda didn't get home until 6:45 that night. Court had run late because of a father who was denied joint custody of his two daughters and ended up being found in contempt of court and detained. After all of that, she'd missed almost every traffic light on the way home. As she walked up the four porch steps, the loose cuff of her uniform's olive green pant leg dragged against the concrete.

"Dang it," she said to herself. She was tired, but the glint of the silver case caught her attention. Brenda tried not to act too excited. All her neighbors with the exception of two had lived on the block for over twenty-five years. They were old and nosy and they knew everyone's comings and goings. Quickly, Brenda checked the windows and security screen doors for neighborly shadows before pulling the case from its hiding place.

Brenda had a schedule, but tonight would be different. Usually when she got home, the first thing she did was place her keys on the first hook on the side of the kitchen cabinet, take the small aluminum pot from the dish holder, fill it with exactly eight ounces of water, and place it on medium heat to boil. Boiling at a lower temperature gave her four minutes to hang up her uniform and holster and change into her gown.

Tonight, she changed into a bright tangerine, extra small, long-leg-length jogging outfit with a matching tank top she had bought from BeBe Sport. Never in her life had she paid so much for a sporting outfit, and never in her life had she been more pleased when she looked in the mirror. She looked thin and hip. The light brown weave made her look contemporary.

She placed the picture of her parents from before she was born, her police academy group graduation picture, and a picture of her, Shay, Shaundra, and Karina from junior high school face-down on the coffee table and moved it out of the way to make room for the pole. Sitting on the recently shampooed living room carpet, the same carpet that had been in her mother's house for twenty-odd years, she opened up the case. All of the pieces were metal and shiny. Brenda lifted one of the pole halves into her hand and noticed Shay's fingerprints. She wondered how many times Shay had actually practiced on the pole and if she'd worked on techniques she'd learned from the class Brenda had not been invited to.

"How do you assemble a pole without directions?" she said after taking each piece out of the case. There were no directions, just a little yellow Post-it note from Shay that read: *Sorry for being an ass. Luv you, sis.* Shay must have forgotten to put the instructions back in the case. That pissed Brenda off. She crawled from her hands and knees to her feet and headed into the kitchen. If she hadn't been so stubborn, she would have called Shay and asked her how to assemble it over the phone. "Humph," Brenda said under her breath as she removed the pot from the stove; a white evaporation ring had formed around the rim from it staying on the fire too long.

She didn't need anyone's assistance; she would figure it out herself, she decided. This would be a solo venture. She smiled. *I'm really going to be a stripper,* she said aloud. None of her friends would have believed her if she had told them, and if they finally realized she was serious, they would have all tried to talk her out of it.

Since she had the pole for only ten days, time of the essence and she needed to figure out where to put it. She looked through each room. The house was small, and one of the two bedrooms was still packed with a lot of her mother's old stuff, which Brenda could never quite convince herself to give away or put in the garage. The only logical place for her to put the pole would be the center of the living room. If she pushed the coffee table and the couch in front of the fireplace, that would give her more than enough room to practice. She glanced around the room again. She had browsed Pier One online during one of her lunch breaks and noticed a mirrored panel divider. It was too expensive, but she was going to get it. She would place it in front of the window to block her neighbors' views and use it perfect her dance movements.

She tried not to think about it, but she was still disappointed that Shay and Shaundra hadn't invited her to the class. Fortunately, she had ordered *Pole Dance 101* and *The 50 Best Lap Dance Moves* online the same night she'd ordered her masks. She was still waiting on her costume accessories, but the DVDs had arrived a few days before. Brenda wasn't the greatest dancer, but this way, she could learn and practice at her own pace.

As she assembled the pole, she wondered what her mother would think about her right now if she were still alive. It saddened Brenda to know that her mother would have been disappointed. Her mother wasn't the most religious woman in the world, but she always went to church on Sundays and at least one day during every revival. Her mother figured it was her just and reasonable service. Just like it had been her just and reasonable service to provide Brenda's father with one child. Brenda had lived her life much the same way, always identifying her reasonable and expected duties. She knew, in her mother's way of thinking, it was Brenda's responsibility not to embarrass or bring shame to her parents. But then again, why should she be worried about the expectations of a deceased mother and a father who had always loved *Playboy* and *Hustler* magazines? These thoughts were the things that made her feel dirty. As much as she never wanted her coworkers, friends, or neighbors to know what she was up to, she knew in the deepest part of herself that she could deal with any disdain they placed upon her. She prayed it wouldn't happen, but she could deal with losing her job if it ever came to that. She needed to branch out. She needed to explore the other parts of herself. Maybe then she wouldn't be such an outsider. Maybe then she would finally have a long-term boyfriend and start a family. Whatever the result, she had to try. And she wasn't going to worry about anything else right now. She had a lot of work to do.

14

A few days after dropping the pole off at Brenda's house, I had made my decision. I wasn't going back to school and I wasn't about to have a baby either. I was about to give birth to an erotic novel series: several books following the lives of my crazy, sex-hungry characters. I wasn't a sexpert. I'd only had sex with two men in my entire life, but I knew what turned me on. And if nothing more, I had an active imagination and that had to count for something.

The series would be titled *Red*. That much I knew so far. I also knew that Marcus, at least at this stage, didn't need to have any idea what I was doing. At the very least, he would stifle me. Worst-case scenario, he would rebuke me and make me stop. That's why I talked to Brenda about setting up my own user identity and password so that Marcus couldn't invade my privacy. As a second-ary precaution, she also showed me how to make myself the com-puter administrator so that Marcus couldn't pull a sucker punch and find out on the sly.

I was ready. Since mystery was at the heart of my fantasy life, I decided that my main characters wouldn't know each other's names, at least not for now. Anonymity would be their catalyst for lust. *Lust*—what a powerful word, I thought. I wanted to scream, I was so excited. This was definitely the most important thing I'd done since high school. Typing *Mistress Writer* into my user ID gave me the same feeling as walking across the podium and collect-ing my diploma. I was on a roll, and I hadn't even started yet. I watched the Microsoft Word license screen flash in front of me, then a blank white screen titled *Document1*. I clicked *File*, then *Save As*. I typed in *RED Chapter One by Shoshannah Cole-Gaines*.

15

"I thought you had Brandi this weekend?" I said loudly from my prime seat on the couch. Unwritten rule or not, Shaundra *always* got the couch. Not tonight. I splayed my lovely self across the couch, shoes off, legs extended to the last cushion.

Shaundra walked out of the kitchen with a large dish of shredded beef lasagna in her hand and the first of many batches of pomegranate margaritas. A look of shock registered on her face. "I know you are not trying to take the queen's couch."

"Umm, I had forgotten just how comfortable this couch is. I haven't sat on it in so long." I took her purple throw from the back of the couch and placed it over my feet.

"Straight up, crackhead," Shaundra said, putting the tip of her finger in the margarita pitcher, then flicking at me.

"Okay, heffa. Don't start nothin', won't be nothin'," I said. I was feeling good. Two hours before, I had just finished the first chapter of my novel. It was short and sweet with a tinge of nasty, just the way I wanted it to be. Walking on air shouldn't be so damn easy. "Where's your trifling sister?" I asked.

Shaun would usually at least give me a look, at least pretend like she was defending Niecee. She just slapped my feet, then pulled her purple afghan off me and sat down.

"I knew your ass didn't know how to share," I said, really a little pissed off. It was her couch and all, but damn, I hadn't sat on the damn thing but once or twice since I went with her to the Specialty Boutique to pick it out.

She leaned forward to start building her plate of lasagna. "Niecee and Brandi's asses are both gone. I sent Brandi to her grandmother's house since James acted like it would have killed him to take her for a couple of days. I was gonna hurt that girl."

I was hungry. I snatched up a plate and got ready to take the serving spoon out of Shaun's hand the second she let go. "Unh-uh, what did my godchild do now?" I said, grabbing the spoon.

Shaundra leaned back. She took a quick bite from her plate. "Girl, this is off the chain. My special sauce and the shredded beef make all the difference. It's perfect. My inner Italian is in rare form."

"Brush your shoulders off," I said. "You still haven't told me what she did."

"Her little ass thought that she was going to walk out of my house in a shirt that said *I go both ways* with an arrow across the breasts that goes in both directions."

"You're lyin', girl." The lasagna was banging. "Who the hell did she get that from?"

Shaundra looked me in the eye and paused. "Niecee." She waited for my reaction.

I slapped the fork to my plate. "You are straight lyin', Shaundra. She didn't let Brandi borrow that shirt. Nuh-unh."

Shaundra remained calm and collected. "They hid it behind her books in her backpack with a micro miniskirt that would have barely cleared Brandi's booty. Oh yeah, and some fishnets. The real kind that really feel like net."

All I could do was shake my head. I didn't even feel hungry anymore. Now I needed a drink. I reached for the pitcher.

"Pour me one, too," Shaundra said. "I don't know what to do. I am so close to stomping a hole in the two of them. I can't live like this. I let Niecee come back to live with me because her situation wasn't working out, and she is trying to make my daughter a ho."

I handed Shaundra a glass. "She ain't trying to make her a ho, Shaun; Niecee *is* a ho and she doesn't know how to act like anything but." The words came out of my mouth a little too honestly. I didn't mean to call Niecee a ho in front of Shaundra, but I wasn't lying. Shaun didn't get mad, which surprised me.

"Girl, I'm at a loss. I don't even know." I looked Shaundra in the face. She looked tired, and her voice sounded deflated.

This must have been what was bothering her the day I picked up the pole. I was glad she was finally talking.

"I'm not trying to come between you and Niecee, Shaun. I know y'all have a complicated relationship. But, Shaundra, you gotta remember what happened the last two times she came to live with you. The shit doesn't ever work out. Lewis. Carl. I'm not trying to be the bearer of bad news, but if you really like Paul, if I were you, I would get Niecee out of my house. . . . It's only a matter of time." I felt bad saying it, but I wouldn't have been Shaun's best friend if I didn't.

Shaundra wouldn't look at me. She pretended like she'd noticed something in her food. "Niecee isn't like that anymore, Shay. Besides, that was years ago."

"You know what they say about a leopard changing its spots. A ho is not a respecter of persons. Not even her sister, or her sister's man."

"That's out of line, Shay." Her voice was still deflated. "Niecee is *still* my sister."

"I'm not trying to clown, Shaun. Unless you make her leave, eventually something is going to happen. I just feel it."

"Well, Paul's never here with Niecee by himself. I usually don't even have him over unless I know Niecee is going to be gone. We stay in my bedroom anyway."

I sipped my margarita. "Nothing might happen with Paul, Shaun. I know that you and Paul are really working it out. But, just like this shirt situation, something else could happen with Brandi. Niecee ain't crazy, but she ain't wrapped like the rest of us."

Shaundra wrung her fingers. "It's not that easy. She's had my back; I just can't make her leave like that. I forgot the tortilla chips in the kitchen. I'll be back."

Shaundra wasn't going to make me feel bad for telling her the truth. But I did feel bad. I knew Shaundra was going to the bathroom to cry. I didn't like any of it, but how do you let your very best friend know that someone who used to have her back, doesn't have it anymore?

I heard a knock on the door. "Whew, saved by the bell," I said to myself. I walked over to the door with margarita in hand and looked through the peephole. It was Brenda.

"Hey, girl," I said, opening the door.

"Hey, Momma," Brenda said as she forged past me with a stoneware dish covered in foil.

"What's that?" I said as I closed the door.

"Chili con queso."

"Oh, good." I sat back down on the couch. "We have something to dip the chips in now; I didn't get a chance to make the shrimp guacamole."

Brenda removed her hot pink scarf and jacket. "What had you so busy today?"

Her question took me by surprise. I thought about saying something about the new book I was starting, but changed my mind. I didn't want to jinx it. "Oh, Marcus called me at the last minute and said he wanted a T-bone with sautéed spinach and I didn't have either one in the house. Then I ended up going to Costco and decided to do the grocery shopping for next week. You know how it goes."

"Not really, but handle yours."

Brenda's mouth was getting progressively smart. "Well, the avocados and raw shrimp are in the kitchen if you get an itch," I said.

She didn't reply.

"Shaun's in the bathroom, and Karina had to work late, so she'll get here when she can." My margarita was getting good to me. I poured another half a cup into my glass. "You're late," I said, stating and asking at the same time.

"I was finishing up a workout and it took a little longer than I expected."

"Oh, yeah, how's the pole working for you? Have you used it yet?"

"A little" is all she said. Instead of her taking her normal place on the love seat, where she generally passed out after two sips of alcohol, she pulled a Karina and sat down on the floor with her legs in a V.

I stared her up and down, like only a good friend can do without getting cursed out. "Your workout fit is kinda tight. When did you start working out?"

She bucked her eyes the slightest bit. "If you must know, a few weeks ago. Is that okay?"

I curled my feet under my butt. Brenda was really trying to get live with me. One part of me wanted to laugh, the other part wanted to snatch her ass. "Girl, I think that is just lovely," I said. "I should start working out again. Maybe when I get my next rotation I'll buy an instructional tape or something."

"Yeah, regular exercise is good for you; especially before you start putting out babies."

I wanted to shoot her a nasty look, but I didn't want to give her the satisfaction. "You about to stretch?"

"Yeah, I think I am."

"I'm gonna get some bowls for this chili stuff you made. Be back." I got up. Whoever this fake-haired Brenda was, I wasn't sure I liked her. The quiet, sweet Brenda had worked just fine for me.

In the kitchen, I bent down to get five petite porcelain bowls from under the counter. From the faint dust resting in the top bowl, I could tell Shaundra hadn't used these bowls in a while. I took them all to the sink. As I washed, I heard keys in the door between the kitchen and garage. Niecee came into the kitchen and slapped her keys on the counter next to the flour and sugar canisters.

"What's up, heffa," she said.

"I thought we were going to be graced *without* your presence this evening."

I have no doubt that she would have flicked her hair if it wouldn't have been in a ponytail. She smiled. "Naw, I wouldn't miss hanging out with my best girlfriends for the world."

She was almost funny. We hadn't had a gathering without Niecee in so long, I wondered if I would have missed her drama. The sickest part of me really wanted to hear what she was going to have to say about Brenda's new hair. I was drying the last bowl when Shaundra came out of the bathroom. She ignored me and looked at Niecee.

"I thought you were going to be gone for the evening."

Niecee took off her black zip-down sweater to reveal the *I go both ways* wife-beater, which she sported with jeans and a baby blue rhinestone belt that complemented the writing on the shirt. "I changed my mind. Decided I wanted some shredded beef lasagna. Besides, I would have missed y'all. Y'all my girls, you know." Niecee smiled brilliantly and made her way to the living room.

I picked up the bowls and walked over to Shaundra. I spoke in a low tone. "Ignore her, Shaun; she's just trying you. Besides" — I patted her arm — "it's a damn shame that we are the closest thing to friends she has."

Shaundra smirked.

"Come on, girl, by the time we get through another pitcher of margaritas, Niecee won't even matter."

I grabbed the bowls, and Shaun took the second pitcher from the freezer. A superficial layer of ice was formed over the top of the reddish-pink liquid.

"When did you get here, Karina?" Shaundra said, placing the pitcher on the coffee table.

"A couple of minutes ago. Those kids really tried to work my nerves. I might even have half a glass of martini tonight."

"Margaritas," Niecee said with a glass already in her hand, sitting exactly where I had been sitting.

I decided to take my own advice and ignore her. I knew she

saw two glasses in front of the couch—one on my side and one on Shaundra's. She'd sat there on purpose.

I reached across the coffee table, grabbed my glass, and sat on the love seat. "Brenda, did Niecee touch my drink?" I glanced at Niecee; she had a problem with drinking out of other people's glasses.

Brenda was deep into her stretching. "I don't think so," she said, not even looking up.

Niecee laughed. "How would she see me drink out of your glass through all of that horse hair? Brenda can't see shit."

Shaundra cut her eyes at Niecee. "You are not about to start, Niecee. Just stop."

"What? If she looks up and that hair brushes across her eyes, she might go blind. A girl gotta be careful."

"I don't care what she thinks," Brenda said. "She can talk all she wants."

"Not in my house and not tonight."

Shaundra was putting her foot down.

"Keep acting bad, Shaun. You just mad 'cause your daughter loves me more than she loves you. I'm out."

It was clear they were both pissed. I hesitated before I said anything. "Let's all chill on each other. It's been a long day. Shaun, Brandi does not love Niecee more than she loves you, and Brenda, your hair looks really cute. Karina, I'm sorry the kids at the group home got on your nerves." I breathed. "Now, what's our movie for the night?"

"*Players Club*," Shaundra said, sounding as dead as ever.

"All right, let's do this. Us strippers got to hone our game, right? Right," I said, feigning excitement and answering my own question. It was a long day, but it was clearly about to be an even longer evening.

16

The club wasn't at all like she had expected. It wasn't elegant and polished like Fantasia or festive as she imagined Teasers would have been had she actually gone inside and not chickened out. It was stale, kind of like a great-grandmother's house. No, more like underwear worn for too long.

I practiced the booty clap bent over the bathroom sink for an hour a day for this? Brenda almost said aloud. She peeked past the unattended money cage at the narrow front entrance, around the corner. From ceiling to floor the club looked lived-in and abused. Dozens of Budweiser flags were draped limply across the ceiling. Bright-red cracked leather booths with high backs played backdrop to square tables covered with dark red table linens. She noticed that more than one table had folded cardboard under the base to prevent leaning. Brenda thought about it. What more could she really have expected from a place called Tits and Ass — T and A's for short.

The lackluster ambience could actually be a good thing. Maybe she didn't need to be nervous at all. She had dressed to the nines. She'd bought a *real* Carnival costume with blue, yellow, and silver sequins that sculpted her breasts and hips. Her bare stomach was actually starting to show the beginnings of a six-pack. Two packs are better than none, she thought. Her heels were a glassy, dark blue, high and hookeresque. Looked like something Niecee would wear to church. Brenda smirked. She looked perfect. The blue and yellow feathered mask she had on complemented the costume flawlessly down to the glittery silver stones around the eyes. Brenda cinched the belt of her trench coat. Now or never, she thought.

It was two o'clock in the afternoon and the club was dead. Brenda walked quietly over to the stage, careful not to make any noise. The stage wasn't as high up as she had expected it to be; it was just above knee level. She leaned down to touch its surface. It felt like her kitchen floor. White linoleum tile with green diamonds in the middle. When she looked up, the dingy ceiling panels seemed fragile, as if the thin metal frames surrounding each rectangle were barely holding them in place. Where the pole was mounted, it looked like someone had cut a chunk of the panel away and haphazardly covered the hole with a black piece of material that ballooned around the silver pole sticking out from its center. *A mess*, Brenda said to herself.

"Yeah," a male voice boomed from behind the bar. "You tryin' to hook up?"

She turned around. "Yeah," Brenda said, trying not to sound nervous. She hoped *hooking up* meant looking for work and not something else. "You hiring?"

He looked her square in the face. Brenda smiled slyly, feeling a certain amount of game she never knew she had.

"I might like you." He smiled back and poured two shots of Blank whiskey. "You a whiskey girl?"

Brenda loosened the belt on her coat so that a little of her sequin-covered breasts showed. "I'm whatever kinda girl you need."

He laughed and pushed her shot toward her. "Yeah, there's something about you I like."

"Really?" she said, feeling like she was on a date with an older man instead of on a job interview.

"Drink," he said.

Already she knew it was going to burn, but she tossed it back anyway, like she had seen too many times on the late-night movie. The liquor singed the inside of her throat. She had never drunk anything that strong besides Listerine, and that was by accident. She tried to breathe in air through her barely parted lips.

"You want another shot?"

All she could manage to do was shake her head no.

"Good," he said, recapping the bottle. "It's good to see you ain't no lush." He pounded his shot down. "Stay that way. *John-ny!*" he yelled back over his shoulder.

Johnny was younger and taller, a lighter-skinned brother, a shade or two lighter than Brenda.

The older man looked back at Johnny. "Nice girl. Nondrinker. She's looking to hook up."

Johnny walked around the bar and sat at the stool next to her. "What's your name?"

"Mardi Gras," Brenda said.

"I see the theme." He waved his hand flippantly at her mask. "Your real name."

Brenda paused.

"It's gonna be on your W-2's, so you may as well tell me now and get it over with."

"Brenda."

"Brenda." He half-smiled and looked back at the older man. "On my lap."

Her knees locked.

"On my lap," he repeated, this time patting his palms on his thighs.

Brenda put her left hand on his lap and he pulled her up.

"Good girl, let me see what I'm working with." He loosened the belt that was holding her trench partially closed. His hand slipped itself under the blue and yellow sequins onto to her bare breasts.

Brenda jumped.

"Better get used to it," Johnny cooed into her ear. "If you wanna do this, being touched by strangers and pretending you like it is part of the job. Grind on me." Johnny looked back to the man behind the bar again. His hands had made a home around her breasts.

Brenda looked back at the bartender, the solitary witness to this embarrassing event. His face was expressionless. He pushed another shot in her direction.

She shook her head no again, but this time because she didn't want to speak. Brenda closed her eyes to stop the tears. She started to work her behind over his dick. The more she moved, the harder he pushed her down onto him.

"You like this," he said into her ear.

"Yes," she said quietly.

"Tell me then. Say 'I like it, Johnny. You're making my pink pussy wet.'"

Her eyes still closed, she started to speak. "I like it, Johnny, you're making my pink pussy wet."

"You got rhythm. You know how to dance?"

Brenda nodded her head yes.

With one hand on her breast and the other groping her waist, he pulled her down on him three good times. "Good girl." He pushed her up off him and slapped her trench coat–covered ass. "Get here around eight o'clock on Wednesday. Bring your clothes, makeup, combination lock, whatever else, and I'll have a girl show you the ropes."

"Thank you," Brenda said, looking him in the eye, glad she had worn the mask and that her tears had somewhere to run other than just down her face. "Wednesday at eight. I'll be here."

17

I started thinking about dancing and Darius all of the time. Dancing relieved my stress and Darius, well, he increased it. Almost every night for weeks, I had been having dreams about him. Wet dreams. Dreams where he pulled my hair and made me shout things I didn't want to say in front of strangers. That wasn't my thing, at least I didn't think it was, but every morning I would wake up soaked. One morning I woke up calling his name. Marcus asked me what was going on; I told him it was a nightmare.

If I would have had the pole, I could've worked out a little of my sexual frustration. But it was Shaun's turn and she was working on a cowgirl routine for Paul. I knew she wasn't going to let me borrow it. Besides, she'd had a hell of a time getting the pole back from Brenda. On the tenth day by eight P.M., it was supposed to be delivered for the next girl's week, if it hadn't been delivered already. When nine o'clock hit, Shaundra let it pass, thinking that Brenda would drop it off in the morning. The pole never came. When Shaundra tried calling her after work the next day, Brenda wouldn't answer her phone. On the third night, the pole case was sitting behind a hedge next to Shaun's door with a note that said *Sorry, I forgot.*

Since I was already done folding laundry, I decided to do the mature thing and try to get in an hour of writing for the day. Just as I sat down, the phone rang. I didn't know whether to feel saved or interrupted. I checked the caller ID. Shaundra was calling from work.

"Yes, ma'am," I said into the receiver.

"What you doin'?" she said, smacking in my ear.

"Nothin'," I said. "Just finished laundry not too long ago. What are you munching on?"

"Poppycock, girl—this popcorn is good. Anyway, I forgot to tell you. Darius's momma had little Darius run a letter down to my house for you on Saturday, but like I said, I forgot to give it to you."

"It's all right, girl. I know Niecee and Brandi were working your nerves. Niggah ain't saying nothing new no way."

"Well this one is thicker than normal, I don't know. I didn't want to open *your shit*." She muffled the last two words into the phone.

"Thanks for not trying to be a nosy-ass. Appreciate 'cha."

"Anyways," she laughed, "I need to get back to the *plantation*. The letter is at the house if you want to go get it. I think Niecee's lazy ass is home, but you have the key anyway. It's in my room, so if you go, lock my door back, because I don't want Niecee in my stuff."

"Cool, I'll probably pick it up tomorrow or something."

"Talk at you later."

"Later."

Little Darius. No matter how much time passed, I still couldn't get used to that one. How could he go and have a child by Rita? Nothing was wrong with the girl—I went to high school with her, too—but damn. *Rita?* I found myself sitting in front of the computer shaking my head. I was already married to Marcus when I found out. I had been married for a minute. Since Darius's mom lives on Champagne and Shaundra lives on Olive and the streets intersect, no one had to know rocket science to figure it out. Besides, Rita was more than happy to flaunt her butterball stomach. Seemed like she was always sitting in Darius's momma's yard, trying to make the announcement to me and my friends: *Darius is with me now; step off.* I had been off; I jumped off his ass first.

It was one thing for him to get with another girl in between jailbreaks, but to get one pregnant, maybe even on purpose, that was deep. I had gotten married, not pregnant. I know it sounds ass-backwards, especially since I had no intention of ever leaving Marcus, but babies are permanent. You can't take them back with a divorce certificate.

And since I already sound bad, I may as well tell the truth and make myself sound worse. I can't stand that little boy. Funny-looking, cone-headed kid. Big ears like his freckle-faced momma. How could Darius have a little boy who was almost nine years old? And bullshitting aside, he looks just like him. The first time I saw him, he was three and I almost cried right there in the passenger seat. I closed down the computer. I needed to know what the letter said.

When I arrived at Shaundra's, I was glad that I didn't see Niecee's bucket in the driveway. I pulled to the curb and got out. Shaun had been gone for over three hours already, but the house still smelled like eggs and bacon. I figured there might be some leftovers on the stove, but I refrained; I had laid down the hog a minute ago, except for the occasional deep-fried pork chop.

I unlocked Shaundra's room and put my keys on the dresser. Looking up, the first thing I saw was the pole. I don't know why, but I was impressed.

"Go, Shaun," I said aloud.

I had to touch it, just to practice a little. Not to would have been like going to an amusement park and not getting on any of the rides. I slid my right hand down the pole. It felt different; I wondered if it was my imagination. I swung around it a few times like I was playing on a tetherball pole.

"You 'bout to strip?"

She scared the hell out of me. "Oh, hey, I was just picking up my letter."

"I guess Shaun taped the letter to the pole, huh?"

My hands found their way to my hips. "What do you want, Niecee? I'm not about to play with you today." I looked around the room until I noticed the letter on the far nightstand. I walked past the bed to get it.

Niecee walked over to the pole, grabbed ahold, spun in the air, and slid down the pole with her sock-covered feet toward the ceiling and her sweat-covered legs in a V.

"I see you still like hanging from your sister's poles." I grabbed my keys and walked toward the door. I knew my comment was out of line, but I almost couldn't help myself. When I looked back, Niecee was lying on her back with her legs splitting the pole.

"If you want to learn a few things, let me know." Her face was playful, but sincere.

"Next time. Can you vacate the room so I can lock up?"

"It's not like I can't get in without the key." Niecee took her sweet time getting up. She brushed past me when she walked through the doorway. "Really, I'll show you some moves Pastor Mark will love." She giggled.

"Bye, Niecee," I said, locking the door. I showed myself out.

This time, Darius's letter didn't have any decorative trim on the envelope or the letter. It was plain and well stated. I sat in the car at Shaundra's curb, almost convinced.

Shay,
I miss you. I mean really, girl. I think bout you even in my
sleep and it's not always bout sex. Sometimes it's how we used
to split a Coke and a banana. Member that?
I'm not gonna keep begging you, Shay-Shay, but I need to
see you. You the only way I'm gonna get through this. Come
through for me, Shay. Alright? You have to know I'm askin' fo
real. Will you come see your niggah? I ain't never belonged to
nobody but you.

I love you, ma,
Darius

There was a visitor's pamphlet enclosed in the envelope.

"I don't know," I said, staring straight ahead. I looked down the street in the direction of Darius's momma's house. It was four houses out of my visibility, but I knew it was there. I wondered how Mrs. Johnson was doing. A big part of me wanted to stop by, but everything was still too close. It had been twelve years since Darius, and it was still just yesterday. Part of my life had moved on, and the other part, what seemed like the bigger part, was still waiting. What could I have really been waiting for—my jailbird ex-boyfriend to come back to me and make my life complete? As naïve as I could seem at times, that wasn't about to happen.

If I could have asked Mrs. Johnson one question, I would have just wanted to know why she kept sending me Darius's letters. I wouldn't give either of them my address. Shaundra would let her bring them to her house, but she wouldn't let him mail them there. Did Mrs. Johnson bring them because she thought I was still number one in his life, or was it because she was a mother who would do anything for her son, right or wrong? I wanted it to be the first reason. Somehow that might justify my standing connection to him. As I turned the keys in the ignition, I hoped that I was strong enough to stay away.

18

It was Paul's night off, and the two of them had gone to dinner at Black Angus and then to play miniature golf. The last time she'd gone to the Play Palace, Brandi had been six, and the last time she had played a video game, Ms. Pac-Man had just come out. Miniature golf was refreshing. That's what she liked about Paul; he wasn't afraid to think outside of the black man box. You can only do dinner and a movie so many times before you'd just rather the guy leave the date money in your mailbox so you don't have to go through the trouble of doing your hair. That's why she'd cut her hair off in the first place. No man was worth frying, dyeing, and curling for. Short and natural would have to do, and Paul didn't mind it. When she thought about it, he actually seemed to like it. Whenever they sat near each other, on the couch, in the car, in bed, Shaundra would find Paul's fingers massaging her head or rolling a short curl around his finger. *He gets me,* Shaundra would often find herself thinking. That was why she knocked him off so much.

In her entire life, no man had ever gotten so much sex out of her. And no one else had ever made her think about getting a stripper's pole. And as long as she could keep his attention on her and out of the strip club, she would be satisfied.

She hadn't found any stripper's number on him since that time two months ago. Though it wasn't a long time, it was long enough for her to start to relax and start trusting him again. When she had called him on it, all Paul had said was, "It's just a stripper. I tip good." Shaundra almost didn't know what to say; he'd caught her off guard with his forthright reply.

"Why are you going to see strippers when you have me?" she remembered asking.

Paul didn't bite his tongue. "Because I like to chill with a beer and watch nude women. It arouses me."

She clamped her legs closed tight at the ankles. His supply was about to be cut off for the night. She covered herself up with his thin discount sheets and turned to face him. He looked unrushed and undisturbed.

"Have you ever slept with one?" she said, trying to match his cool, collected flow.

"Yeah, one young woman, but I starting dating her before I knew she stripped." Paul just lay there on his back like nothing was wrong and pulled Shaundra's free arm over to his mouth to kiss it. She pulled her arm away with quickness.

"What do you mean, *before you knew?* How the hell didn't you know?"

Paul remained calm. "*Because*"—he threw her a perturbed look—"she told me she worked the late shift at Denny's on Sixty-fifth, and when I showed up one night after work during her shift, she wasn't there. That's how."

She still wanted to be mad. Reason or not. "How long did you date her?"

"A year."

"A *year?*"

Paul turned on his side to face her. "Yeah, Shaun, a year. Why is that so bad?"

"She was a stripper. She took money to please men. That doesn't seem wrong to you?"

"I like to give these women money and be entertained by them. Who am I to judge?"

"Is there any way I can stop you from going?" She kissed his lips like only a woman with full honeysuckle lips can do, and let her Chanel No. 5 linger under his nose.

He kissed her back, and she felt Mr. Bullet rise against her thigh. "I don't know," he said, getting into his groove, "maybe if you did a strip thing for me, I wouldn't even want to go."

That was all he had to say. Within a week of finding that card, she'd ordered her own pole.

Two months has to be a good thing, Shaun said to herself as she watched Paul complete his last hole. They had gone through the entire miniature golf course two times. One time for free because on the last hole when the windmill takes the ball, they skipped that hole and worked the whole course again. It was always a good night with Paul. She was yet to have a really bad one.

"Are we still going to my place?" Paul asked after they got back into his Chrysler Sebring.

Shaundra's sleepover bag was in the trunk and she was all set to spend the night, but something told her she needed to go home. "Baby, why don't we go to my house tonight? I have a little surprise for you."

"You ain't got to convince a brother. Your house it is. Let's just hope your crew is asleep."

They were asleep. At least it seemed that way. Shaundra couldn't see any blue light streaming through the living room curtains from the television; that was a good sign. Because Niecee's and Shaundra's cars were both holding down their respective spots in the garage, Paul pulled quietly into the driveway. Shaundra grabbed her leftover steak and baked potato container, Paul grabbed her bag from the trunk, and they headed up the walkway.

"Shhh," she said as she crouched at the door and slid the key into the lock. The living room was clear. Shaun led Paul through the kitchen to drop off her food. In the hallway she saw blue light under both Niecee's and Brandi's bedroom doors and heard Alan Alda's voice in tandem, which meant they were both watching *M*A*S*H.* A smile graced her lips, and she praised God that all was good in her world. She shut her bedroom door.

"I'm ready for you, baby," Paul said. He lay atop her bed in nothing but his cotton boxers that had little fishermen in boats on them. Shaundra giggled on the inside. How did she ever find him? He had his own strange little ways, but she couldn't see herself asking for a better man. Even if he was a petite guy and she seemed to flank him on every side when they had sex, he knew how to use his tools, and when she closed her eyes, she felt a big man all around her.

"Give me five minutes to freshen up. 'Kay, baby?"

This was Paul's first time being at the house when she had her pole up. "Take your time, woman; I'm just gonna lie here and imagine what you're gonna do on this pole for me. Hot damn!" Paul's voice didn't rise, but she could feel the intensity and desire in his timbre. Her snatch was already starting to get wet.

Shaundra took her gear with her into the bathroom. She set the brown leather chaps, gun holster, leather vest, and reinforced bikini top on the puffy purple seat cover. The edible underwear was still in its package. The silver plastic gun sat atop the lacquered laundry basket. She didn't say it, but she thought it with all her heart: My big ass is going to fuck his brains out. Quietly, of course, so as not to wake anyone.

Paul was usually a pretty calm and contained man, but seeing her, with her breasts bulging out of a too tight vest and her coochie covered in a candy G-string, made his whole body rise up involuntarily. She held his gaze, then turned to expose her fabulous, oiled behind.

"God has been too good to *me*," he said. "God has been *too* good."

Shaundra didn't crack a grin. She was serious about going after her man. In black patent leather six-inchers, she made her way to the pole. She didn't play any music, because she didn't want to interrupt her family—plus, she didn't need any. She grabbed ahold of the stainless steel pole and spun quickly just once. Then she let go and began to move her body in a slow snake.

"Yes, yes, yes-yes-yes," Paul said.

She bent her back, continued rolling her body backward. She unzipped her vest, then took both hands and rubbed them over her almost bald head. When she brought her hands forward over her face, she took her right middle finger and placed it in her mouth. She swirled it around her tongue a few times and pulled it out. As the middle finger cleared her chin and slid down her neck, Paul saw the first traces of a saliva trail making its way down her body. She grazed her breastbone, then her stomach.

"Do you want this wet finger in here?" she said as she pointed down to her crotch.

"Ummm-hmmm," Paul said gutturally.

"Then you're gonna have to lick this off of me." She placed her middle finger inside the edible drawers. Shaundra moved closer to him, and before she made the last two steps to the bed, where she intended to ride his face, Paul dropped himself to his knees. The carpet was plush, but that had to have hurt, she thought. Paul didn't seem at all dazed. He grabbed her bare ass and pummeled into her crotch. His mouth opened wide over her.

"Take this mothafucka, Paul, take this mothafucka before I give the shit away to someone else. This pussy is hot caramel, baby," she almost whispered.

Paul followed instructions. He forced a large hole through the damp panties and licked his tongue down her clit into her vagina. Shaundra grabbed at the air, but there was nothing to hold on to.

"Do it, Paul. Baby, please. Oh, Paul. Fucking shit."

Paul pressed his rounded nails into her ass. She found herself wrapping her arms around the back of his head and gyrating out of control.

"Yesss, baby. Come on my tongue. Let me take this, let me take this."

Shaun was just about to let go on his tongue when she swore she heard low moans coming from outside the room.

"Work that big ass, baby. Work that ass."

Shaundra forced herself to concentrate. She closed her eyes and tried to regain the momentum of the climax that had been knocking at her vaginal walls just seconds before.

She heard it again. This time with more intensity.

"Did you just hear something?" she asked Paul.

"Naw, baby. Nothing, baby. Come on, give me this."

Shaun stood there with her eyes open and her back gaining erectness as Paul worked his tongue maniacally on her pussy. She hated to stop him, but she had to.

"Baby, Paul. One second, baby." She looked down at him and touched his shoulder. The glow of the nightstand lamp highlighted the sweat and frustration on his face.

"What's going on, baby?" He got up from his knees, exasperated. He sat back on the bed with both hands resting on his hard dick, which had made its way through the slit of his fisherman boxers.

Shaundra cut into mommy mode. She rushed to the bathroom to grab her robe from the back of the door. "I don't know," she said quietly. "I don't know, but I know something is going on. I think Niecee brought some niggah up in my house around my daughter."

Shaundra tied a knot with her robe belt, her chaps showing below the bottom of the purple Egyptian cotton.

"You want me to go check?" Neither Paul's voice or his expression seemed convincing.

"I got it," Shaundra said, sensing her first inkling of frustration with him. She took her role of mother seriously, and yes, it was more important than a good nut.

When she entered the hall, the voices seemed a little more ethereal, like they were coming from two places at once. Shaundra didn't need any more proof. She knocked on Niecee's door.

"Open the mothafuckin' door, Niecee. I am not playing. I have fucking had it this time."

Niecee took her time; she always took her time. A full minute later, Niecee snatched the door open.

"What?" she said, full of attitude, her arms crossed squarely over her powder-blue tank she wore above matching blue panties.

Shaun matched her attitude and called her one. "What the fuck was that?"

Niecee bucked her eyes and gave her the here-we-go-now expression. "What was what?"

"I'm not playing, Niecee. I heard it. You got a niggah in there?"

"Get the fuck out of my face, Shaun." She turned and started to close the door.

Shaundra pushed the door open and followed her into the room.

"You better get up off me, Shaun, before I hurt you." Niecee seemed calm, like she always used to seem when they were kids before she swung a good one on Shaundra. Niecee's violence seemed to come from a place of peace and resolution, not fear.

"You ain't hurting shit in my house. This is my mothafuckin' house, in case your homeless ass forgot." Shaundra moved quickly. She bumped past Niecee and lifted the edge of the comforter to look under the bed, then headed toward the closet.

Niecee rolled her eyes at Shaundra's back. "You ain't gonna find nothing, Shaun. Not unless you are looking for this." Niecee crawled onto the bed as Shaundra continued to search the closet. When Shaundra finished her search and came up empty-handed, she looked back at Niecee. Niecee held a white vibrator with a lime-green prickly nub on top. Niecee sat on the bed while Shaun digested the moment. Niecee stared Shaundra in the eye.

In all her days of living, Shaundra had never felt so out of control. She would have killed Niecee, she swore to herself she would have. She pressed her palms to her eyes and breathed hard. She had to get ahold of herself. This constant mistrust of everyone in her household wasn't working.

"I just, um, I ah—"

Niecee smirked. "You just forgot what the sounds of self-pleasure sound like, since you got a man now. Big ol' strapping Paul."

"Paul's in the room, Niecee." She spoke in a low tone, but authoritatively. "Don't disrespect him."

Niecee lifted both of her hands in exclamation. "I don't care if his ass is standing in the hallway. I don't understand how you screw your man in this house almost every other night and I can't even have a niggah up in the house for more than five minutes. Hilarious," she said, feigning laughter.

Shaundra was exhausted, yet at the same time relieved the worst wasn't before her. "Niecee, I'm sorry for interrupting your private time. That wasn't my intention. When you get a regular man, and you want the privilege of having him spend the night, you need to move in with him or get your own apartment." She walked toward the door. "I'm not trying to disrespect you or anything. These are just my rules. Do you want me to close your door?"

Niecee flicked her hair and turned over. "Get the fuck out."

Shaundra closed the door. As she walked down the hall back to her bedroom, it occurred to her that Brandi had probably heard everything and thought that big, bad momma was being too hard on Auntie Niecee again. She turned around. The blue light was still coming from under Brandi's door, but the volume had been turned completely down. Shaundra rapped on the door lightly. No answer. Shaundra knocked again.

"Brandi, you asleep?"

No answer.

"Brandi, I know you heard us and I know you're mad. Talk to me." She squeezed her voice through the space where the door and the frame met.

Nothing.

She tried the door. Locked. "Brandi, open up."

Finally she heard Brandi's voice. "No, Mom, I'm fine. Let's talk tomorrow."

"Brandi, I'd much rather talk now. I don't want you going to sleep mad at me. This whole situation is bigger than it seems. I'm not trying to ride your Auntie Niecee."

Brandi's voice came muffled through the door again. "*Really*, I'm not mad. Can you just give me a little space for the night? Please?"

Shaundra felt defeated. There was no point in constantly fighting upstream. "I'm not going to fight you, Brandi. You come to me when you want to talk. I'm tired of this craziness."

She left the door and went back to her room. Paul had arranged himself comfortably under the covers. She crawled into bed next to him with her robe, chaps, vest, bikini, and half-eaten edible panties on.

"Tough one?" He kissed her forehead.

"Yeah," she said, feeling completely deflated.

"It's going to be all right, Shaundra. I know what a good mother you are. My ex-wife, she may not have been the greatest wife in the world, but she is a wonderful mom. I feel the same way about you."

Shaun knew he intended the whole comparison as a compliment, so she didn't sweat him. She looked him in the eyes, and his sincerity actually made her feel better.

"You actually think I'm a good mother?" She was still staring at him.

"Yes, and unlike my ex-wife, I think you are the perfect woman for this big strapping man."

Shaundra smiled. "You heard Niecee. She was just trying to make me mad and make her point." Shaundra rubbed his head. She could feel little pricks from his hair starting to grow back. "I'm lucky to have you," she said, wanting to say more, but not wanting to give away too much at one time.

He pushed away from her a little, as if to refocus and get a better look. "You trying to say you love me, woman?"

In her worn-down state, she figured she didn't have anything else to lose. You have to take a chance sometime, she told herself.

Shaundra stared deeply into his eyes. There was nothing that told her she shouldn't. "Yes, I love you, Paul."

He kissed her lips, this time letting his tongue linger for a second. "I love you too . . . Amazon woman."

Shaundra really needed this. "You are crazy, Paul."

He kissed her deeply this time and gathered his arms around her so that his hands pressed her back and pressed her into him. "You down for round one and a half?"

"Yeah, just let me do one quick thing first. I forgot to tell my daughter that I love her."

Shaundra walked down the hall feeling lighter. Before she knocked on the door again, it occurred to her to pause first. She heard her daughter's voice. But she also heard another voice that wasn't Niecee's.

"Brandi, open this door," she screamed.

Dead silence.

"Brandi Lynn, if you make me go get my keys, I swear I'm going to beat your black ass."

Niecee opened her door so fast, Shaundra could feel the rush of air. "Why don't you leave the girl alone? Haven't you already been a big enough lunatic for the night? Hell, I would run away if I was her."

"It's not your business. Paul, bring me my keys, please."

"I'm half dressed and you're telling your man to come out here?"

"Hurry, Paul."

He grabbed her keys and only glanced at Niecee for a second before he turned all his attention to Shaundra. She grabbed the keys, but her hand was shaking too badly for her to get the door open. Paul, still in his boxers, took the keys from Shaundra and opened the door.

Tears came to Shaun's eyes when she saw a young boy standing in Brandi's room. Paul felt her take off toward Brandi and grabbed her before she could get through the door right.

"I am going to kill you, Brandi. I swear to God Almighty.

Paul, let go of me!" She wrestled to get loose. Paul kept his hold.

The young man had stepped in front of Brandi to protect her.

"Oh, shit," Niecee said, knowing that it was really about to hit the fan.

"Who the fuck is this?" Shaundra still tried to get away from Paul.

"Derrick. . . . My boyfriend."

"Let me go, Paul, I swear to God. Let me go."

Niecee crossed her arms over her chest. "Ain't no use in getting all bent. It ain't gonna change nothing. The girl's got a boyfriend."

"What the fuck is he doing in my house?" Shaundra looked to Niecee, then to Brandi.

Brandi smacked her lips. "He was just leaving."

Shaundra played it calm for a second then tried to make a fast break through Paul's arms. Both Brandi and the boy flinched. "*He was just leaving?* What the fuck was he doing here?"

Brandi was silent. She looked at the carpet.

"What was he doing here, Brandi?"

Niecee rolled her eyes. "Let the girl alone, Shaun," she repeated again.

"Answer me, Brandi."

"Dang, Momma, we was just doing what kids our age do, that's all."

Shaundra looked closely at the two of them. They were both fully dressed. Brandi in a T-shirt, shorts and socks, the boy in a Sean John button-up shirt, shoes, and jeans, with his zipper undone.

Shaundra shook her arms. "Unh-uh. Let go of me, Paul," she said matter-of-factly.

"Are you sure, woman? You don't want to do anything you are going to regret."

"Let go of me," she said softly.

Paul loosened his grasp.

"What *do* kids your age do?"

Brandi wouldn't say anything. It seemed like she and the boy were concentrating on the same spot on the carpet.

Shaundra's voice sounded quizzical. "Coitus? Is that what kids your age do? Fuck?"

Brandi spoke up boldly, like she was tired of hiding. "Yes, Mom, that's what kids my age do. We have sex. Nothing is wrong with that. We use condoms. At least me and Derrick do, anyway."

Derrick grabbed Brandi's hand. "It ain't like you ain't gettin' none. You got a stripper's pole in your bedroom, Momma."

The burning in her throat spread to Shaundra's heart. She tried to suck some air into her lungs. She didn't understand how her little girl had turned into such a trifling little wench. Shaundra held her hand to her mouth, though she hadn't actually said anything.

"Get out," she said to the young boy. "Get out of my house."

The boy looked at Brandi then Niecee, then over to Shaundra. "I'm sorry, Ms. Owens."

Shaundra wiped the latent tear from her face with the lapel of her robe. "Why are you sorry? Hmmm? You got exactly what you wanted. You turned my daughter into a little slut." She wiped away the snot from her nose with the back of her hand. "See, I just called my daughter a slut and I'm not sorry. Make your actions mean exactly what you want them to. Once you put them out there, you can't take them back. You came over to my house in the middle of the night to fuck. You got what you wanted. Don't apologize to me. Get out."

"Niecee, can I still get a ride home?"

Shaundra looked at Niecee, and before anyone knew it, she had jumped on top of her. After she slapped the hell out of her, she went for her hair. "You knew about this? You knew my daughter had a boy in her room? You knew she was having sex in my house?"

Paul grabbed Shaundra off her, but Shaun tried her best to keep ahold of Niecee's hair.

Niecee wiped her mouth with her palm, then looked at it, checking for blood.

"You're not a woman, Niecee. I don't know what you are, but you ain't no woman. And you're not my sister. Shay, Brenda, and Karina are better sisters than you."

"Don't talk to her like that," Brandi chimed in.

"When you take this boy out of here tonight, you need to take your shit as well, because I don't want you living in my house anymore."

Brandi let go of Derrick's hand and ran over to wrap herself around Niecee. Brandi started crying. "You can't make her leave, Momma. Please." She cried into Niecee's powder-blue chest. "If she leaves, I am going with her."

Shaundra knew she didn't mean what she was about to say, but hurt was talking louder than love. "The more the merrier. All you Negroes can get to steppin'."

"You don't mean that, Shaundra," Paul said, trying to catch her eye. When he finally made eye contact, he could see the hurt all over her face.

"Yes I do, Paul. I'm done."

Niecee's face was the only face that was dry. "I'm leaving your damn house, but I will say this. At least Brandi is having sex with a boy she wants to have sex with, instead of a grown man to keep a roof over her sister's head, like I did for you. Shay and Brenda and them are better sisters to you than I am, huh?" Tears finally started to well up in Niecee's eyes. "None of them would have done for you what I did. I made sure he didn't touch you. But I was touched, Shaundra. I was touched the whole time she was gone."

"Let's go, Paul. Let's go." Shaundra finally walked away, like she had been trying to do for her entire life.

19

Even though Johnny had felt her up, she knew this was just the beginning. She looked at herself in the scalloped mirror attached to her dresser and said to her reflection, "You don't have to go through with this. You've proven that you have the balls to go after what you want, Brenda."

She continued to pack her bag, which already contained two costumes and makeup. She went into the bathroom to get her deodorant and a hand towel, then looked at herself again. She had on a plain, fitted jogging suit and her hair was in a ponytail. She looked like she was going to the park or to get the tires changed on her car. Nothing special. Nothing out of the ordinary. She shook out her hands a couple of times to calm the nervousness, then placed her 9mm Beretta, holster, and loaded magazine with fifteen bullets in the side of the bag. She zipped the bag shut. Her gun was work issued, and if anything went down, she would have a lot of explaining to do, but she felt safer having it with her; it was something that she'd have access to off duty anyway. This would be the first time in over nine years that she would go to work without a gun on her hip. Her stomach was in a knot.

About two miles from the club, Brenda turned off the freeway and stopped in the Circle K parking lot. She pulled to the side of the building and took her mask from its case. Brenda closed her eyes, pulled the band around her head, and adjusted the holes around her eyes. She was set. Mardi Gras was on her way.

Arriving at the club, she didn't give herself time to chicken out. As soon as she turned the engine off, she pulled the key out of the ignition and headed around the car to grab her bag. She passed an array of people on her way in. Most of them looked homeless or like prostitutes, or both.

This time when she approached the money cage, she saw that there was a woman in it. She waited in line behind two customers before she got the chance to speak.

Brenda spoke loudly to hear herself over the background noise. "Hi, I'm Mardi Gra—"

"I know, I know," the woman said into the microphone. "You're new. Welcome to the bottom. Go on in and Johnny or someone will get you situated."

"Thanks," Brenda said.

When she turned the bend, the first thing she noticed was that the club was crowded, unlike the first time she'd come. The bass from the bump-and-grind music seemed to be bouncing from wall to wall. She walked through the crowd of primarily men, trying to make sure her bag didn't get caught on anyone. The only people she knew were Johnny and the bartender, so she headed toward the bar trying to find the bartender first. As she crossed the club, the woman on the stage caught her attention. She was a dark brown sistah with more bootyliciousness than Brenda had actually ever seen on a live person. The only part of her thong that was visible was a pink band; the rest was hidden between her butt cheeks. When she finally got past the ass to the bare breasts with darker brown areolae around the nipples, Brenda's stomach knotted. This was going to be her, in a matter of minutes for all she knew. She wanted to turn around and run out, but somehow her body kept moving forward.

Edward, the bartender, spotted her first. "Hey, Catwoman," he yelled out with enough force to catch her attention. *Catwoman*, she replayed in her head. All of her newly found bad-girl attitude was flying out of the window; she was plain scared.

"Hi," she said. Brenda watched him pour an amber liquor into what looked like Coke.

"I see you still have your disguise on." He looked up at her and nodded toward her mask.

She didn't realize her reasoning was so obvious. "It's a part of my persona," was all she could think to say.

Edward laughed. "*Persona.* I can tell you weren't raised in the hood. Down here it is called a disguise."

She didn't say anything. She had remembered him as much nicer a few days before.

"Where do I go?"

He collected money from the bar counter, then looked around. "Splendid. *Splendid!*" The woman looked over at him. "Yeah, you. Come over here."

Splendid walked over and slapped her hand on the counter. "What the fuck, Ed, I'm trying to get a dance. What?"

Edward ignored her attitude. "She's new. Take her back and show her where to place her stuff."

"This *ain't* part of my job. You owe me a screwdriver."

"Screwdriver your ass on back to the pit and let me do *my* job."

Splendid rolled her eyes and walked away. She'd made it a few steps before Brenda's legs kicked into gear and started to follow her.

"I'll be back in five minutes," Splendid said loudly to a customer and smoothed her hand down his leg as she passed.

Brenda followed her out of the noise of the club into a long hallway that led to a room that looked like a gigantic women's locker room.

"You new to dancing?"

"Yeah," Brenda said.

"Figured as much." Splendid rolled her eyes. "This is the Pit," she said, her hands spilling a dry voilà gesture into the air. "Find any locker that don't already have a lock on it and it's yours. You can leave shit in it overnight, but if I were you, I would take all my shit home when I leave, 'cause shit can disappear. If you didn't bring a lock, you better pray over it or something, and put your purse in the car."

Brenda nodded, glanced around at the other three women in

various stages of dress, then spotted a locker a few steps away. "I brought a lock," she said.

"What else?" Splendid flicked her hair. She reminded Brenda of Niecee. "Sometimes the order switches, so when you know you're supposed to be up in a coupla songs or something, stay on deck so you don't miss your spot. If you miss your spot, you get a fine and that's some bullshit. This place looks a hellhole, and really it is, but it runs kinda like the fuckin' military."

Brenda nodded.

"Also, give the DJ your song sheet as soon as you know what you want to dance to and make sure he has the music, otherwise he'll substitute some shit and fuck up your routine. He'll let you know your *real* order."

"All right," Brenda said. The flash tutorial was making her more nervous.

"Depending on how many girls show up, you can probably dance at least two sets a night, on weeknights maybe three or four. After each dance, count out at the counter behind the stage. You only tip out every time you hit a hundred dollars, which is pretty fair. You have to hit up your bouncer and the DJ. And on the real, if Ed treats you good at the bar, you might wanna tip him in, too."

"Okay," Brenda said in blind agreement.

Splendid adjusted her breasts in the mirror. "First dance is with your top on, the second number is always topless. No bottoms off by law, but if you want to show a little twat, you always make a little more money that way. Just push your thong to the side. You won't get a fine for that. I think that's it. Everybody shares the mirror stations. Anything else?"

Brenda placed her bag carefully on the bench in front of her. "I don't think so."

"Really work it good your first couple weeks. The niggahs pay good for new ass, but once they get used to you, you gotta work for every fucking dollar you get. And no matter how many signs say No Strippers Sitting at the Bar, if a niggah offers you a free drink, sit your ass down and take it. Everybody does it and drinks are expensive as fuck."

"Thanks for the breakdown."

"That's okay. You owe me a drink. What's your name?"

"Mardi Gras."

Brenda unzipped her bag, careful to keep her holster covered. She fought the urge to glance out of the corner of her eye; she didn't want anyone to think that she was staring at them. She had never liked undressing in front of people. She used to especially hate it in junior high and high school. Brenda took out her blue sequined thong, skirt, halter, and heels. She felt the urge to go change in the bathroom, but what was the point of being shy anymore? She was about to become a stripper.

She unzipped her sweat top and then removed her pants. Her old-school white bra with thick adjustable straps and her tan full-bottomed panties seemed completely out of place. She sat down on the bench before she dropped her tan drawers. She jumped up a little to get them past her butt, then rolled them down her legs. She put the thong over her feet and rolled it up in similar fashion.

When she was completely dressed, she didn't look like anyone she knew. The real Brenda was gone as far as she could tell. She stared at herself in the mirror, knowing that there was still a big possibility that she would chicken out. She relined her lips with a chocolate Maybelline eyebrow pencil, then sat at the mirror station to do her eyes. As a street officer and then as a bailiff when she changed branches, the eyes were always what made her trust a person's story, or they were what gave that person away.

"You just gotta do it," a voice said from behind.

Brenda looked back. She was a pretty girl. Thin face, hair that cut just below her ears.

"The first time is always the hardest, but really, you'll get used to it."

"I'm not sure," Brenda said, feeling like it was the first honest thing she had said in weeks. "This might not be for me."

The girl took the chair from the next station and sat down. She only had a sunset orange thong on and no bra or blouse, but she seemed completely comfortable. "Stripping ain't for nobody. It's hard on a sistah, even a ho. Hold up a second."

Brenda couldn't even think straight. She shouldn't even have started this process. She wasn't a stripper. She hadn't even had a real boyfriend in almost five years; how was she supposed to go out there and pretend to be sexy?

"Look," the girl said, sitting back down in her chair. "This is my personal reserve, so don't say shit or they'll fine me." She handed Brenda her cup.

Brenda could tell, without even leaning down to smell it, that it was alcohol. Straight. Without anything to kill the sting.

"I don't drink."

The girl leaned over and laughed. Her bare nipples touched Brenda's arm. "Everyone drinks. You either drink, do drugs, or go crazy. Sometimes the thing that seems the easiest costs you the most. Just hammer the vodka back. You'll barely feel anything on stage."

Brenda thought about what she'd said. *The easiest things often cost the most.* Maybe that was the situation of some of the other girls—it was easier to strip than to take a job making half as much and working more hours—but it wasn't until this moment that she truly realized she had something to lose. She had a career and she had built a good respectful life for herself.

She palmed the Styrofoam cup in her hand and hammered it back. The burn was intense.

The girl scooted closer. "Now take this and wiggle it around your tongue and gums. You can spit it out in the bathroom down the hall."

The Listerine tasted as bad as the vodka. Brenda swished it around her mouth a few times, then got up to go the bathroom.

She was already starting to feel a warm comfort on the inside. With the heels on, she felt like she was walking on marshmallows. When she got back to the pit, the girl was in front of her own locker, retying her bikini top. She yelled back at Brenda, "If I were you, I'd go turn in your music list and get in rotation. Thursday is always a good night here. Watch a couple of girls, then just do your thang."

Brenda grabbed her playlist off the mirror station counter, then placed her eyebrow pencil and lipstick back into her locker. It was now or never.

20

I really wanted to talk to Shaundra; she was the only person who would possibly understand. But she wasn't going to understand. I knew that in advance, but I still wanted to talk to her. She knew me. She knew me and Darius together. She knew what I would have given for him back in the day.

She wasn't answering her phone. I had been calling her all morning, at work and at home. It was rare that I didn't touch base with her at least once a day. I sat at my computer desk with the visitors' pamphlet in my hand. I wanted to visit him. I hadn't seen him in so long; I wanted to remember what he looked like. What he smelled like. What it felt like to have his arms around me again.

I was in over my head and I needed my best friend to help save me. Sometimes the only way out is to get help.

I pressed redial. "Shaun, pick up the damn phone," I channeled into the telephone line. I got her work answering machine again. I pressed the cordless receiver between my legs. I had a burning so deep in my flesh I didn't know what to do with myself. I needed to masturbate. Maybe that would get rid of the edge, I thought.

I grabbed the crotch of my sweatpants and felt my flesh tighten. If I'd have been able to reach her, I know what she would have said. *Don't go, Shay. You're only asking for trouble. Would you want Mark to go visit some chick he was still hot for?*

I would have rationalized to her. *He's in prison, Shaun. It's not like we're going to make out or something. Guards are going to be everywhere. And who says I am HOT for him anyway; I haven't seen him in years.*

And then she would have paused on the phone and dropped the killer, the line that was supposed to make me keep my horny, bored ass at home. *Guards will be everywhere but in your mind, Shay. And that's where you need them the most. Darius will mindfuck you, Shay, and you know it. Don't fuck off your whole marriage for some bullshit.*

I would have probably gotten off the phone at that point. What comeback do you have for a breakdown as cold and true as that?

It didn't matter if Darius was still in prison; he wouldn't be forever. He had even told me a few letters ago that his parole hearing was coming up soon.

The devious part of me started to take over again. *Well, he's not out of prison yet, Shaun. Now what?*

I pressed my clitoris with my left hand and fingered through the visitors' pamphlet again. My mind flipped between taking in the information and thinking about the fact that Darius was left-handed. Even as a teenager, he knew exactly what to do to make me feel good. The visiting rules were pretty strict. I would only be allowed to make limited contact at the beginning and end of the visit. I could bring in five dollars' worth of quarters for use at the vending machines. Prisoners with low Detention Center numbers were allowed visits weekend after next. High numbers had hours this upcoming weekend. I pulled Darius's letter out of my folder and looked for his DC number. He was high. I smiled to myself. I could see him this upcoming weekend if I wanted to.

"Baby, what are you so happy about?"

I hadn't heard Marcus come into the house. "Nothing," I said, removing my hand from my crotch and scrambling to get the letter and pamphlet under the folder.

Marcus came over to me and brushed his lips across my forehead. "It has to be something—you're glowing." He kissed the side of my face.

I pushed my folder to the corner of the desk, then rolled my chair around to face him. "I'm just a little happy, that's all. My book is starting to come along."

"Really now." Marcus sat on the corner of the desk, his suited pant leg touching my arm.

"Yeah, I just minutes ago finished my second chapter. Good stuff, I think."

"May I partake?"

I must have looked at him like he had lost his mind. "Marcus? No."

"Come on, Shannah, I won't laugh." He grabbed for my folder.

I slapped his hand, and the pamphlet and letter flew off the front of the desk. I jumped up, walked around the desk, and folded the papers in my hand before he could move.

"What is that, Shoshannah?" he said, his voice taking on the tone of my husband, the pastor.

"Mark," I said, looking completely irritated, but feeling completely scared. "You have to give me a little space. I don't want you reading my book until I am ready for you to read it."

"I just asked you what something is, Shannah. You're my wife. I can't ask you questions?"

"Yes, Mark, but you can't interrogate me. I don't need to talk to you about every piece of mail that I get." As soon as I said it, I knew I shouldn't have.

"Mail? I thought what you dropped had something to do with your book."

"It does, Mark. Aren't I allowed to do research? Or are you just jealous that I am finally doing something with my life and not catering to you 24-7?" As much as I was trying to drop him off my scent, I also wanted to know the answer to my question.

Mark shook his head. "Look, I'm just trying to be involved in your life, Shannah. I came home to surprise you so that we could have lunch together."

"So that I could make you lunch, you mean?" I placed my hand on my hip.

"If you want to make lunch, Shannah, that's fine, or we can go out and grab something."

Man of God that he was, I knew that he was lying. He wanted me to whip something up quick because of course, I didn't have anything else to do.

"I don't have time for that today, Mark. I need to finish my research and start my next chapter." I sat back down at the desk with the papers squished between my legs, hoping he would leave.

Marcus rubbed my shoulder. "I wasn't trying to disrespect your time, Shannah. I just thought it would be nice to have lunch together for a change. I'm teaching Bible study tonight. I'll see you when I get home."

I listened to Mark pick up his keys. Before he opened the door to leave, I was already feeling torn.

21

By the time Shaundra got in the car, she felt like someone had beaten her with a horseshoe. Her ribs felt sore, though no one had actually hit her with anything. She was glad she had slapped Niecee; she wished she had socked her. Her next thought was that she wished she hadn't done anything at all. That was how her thoughts flip-flopped the whole twenty-minute ride to Paul's house. She sat on the passenger side, gazing out the window, his hand on her lap. Though she tried to mask her body language and make it seem like everything was normal, everything was a blur.

She kept thinking: Had she not said anything, she wouldn't feel this bad right now. Had she not even gone home, she would have been completely oblivious. *My sixteen-year-old daughter is having sex,* Shaundra thought sadly. The idea of her daughter opening up to a man the way that she did with Paul did something twisted to her spirit. Brandi having sex seemed unnatural. She should have at least waited 'till college to make a decision like that. Brandi had choices. Solid choices. Way more than either Niecee or Shaundra had ever had growing up. She didn't have to use her body and street-sense to get ahead like they had. And Shaundra was grateful—though she had flirted and teased as a young girl, and gotten into things she wasn't supposed to—she was grateful she had never had to use her body the way that Niecee had.

Paul's apartment was small and manly-esque. It almost looked like a woman had never put a loving touch to it. Shaundra had tried to here and there. She bought a small basket with plastic lemons and oranges for the table in the dining nook. She cleaned the bathroom mirrors and placed potpourri in key spots. She'd rid the refrigerator twice of things in bags that looked like they had died and been reincarnated as green slime. And she always changed the bed sheets every time she slept over. She had done her part as far as she was concerned, but this was Paul's apartment. She reminded herself to keep clear in her mind that she was not Paul's wife.

He wasn't so bad, though. He kept his body clean and orderly, and this was the first man's toilet Shaundra didn't feel the need to sanitize first before she sat her precious behind upon it. Paul was an ex-military man from Kentucky. He'd retired after twelve years and become a supervisor for a bookbinding plant. He was older, but comfortably older, not the nasty kind. Shaundra liked his southern ways and his directness. She'd had a hard time finding good manners and respect in men in their thirties, her ex-husband included.

Shaundra sat on the couch and wrapped herself up in the purple throw she had bought him, the same kind that draped the back of her couch.

"Paul, would you mind turning on the heat some?"

"Naw," Paul yelled from the bathroom, "give me a minute."

"That's fine." Shaundra found her thoughts reaching back to Niecee and Brandi. She wondered what Brandi was doing and if the boy was still in her house. A quake of fear ran through her: Maybe no one was home and maybe they weren't coming back. Shaundra wanted to grab her bag and ask Paul to take her home, but what was that going to solve either way? It would only make the situation worse.

"You want some tea? I have chamomile and vanilla hot chocolate."

Shaundra knew exactly what he had; she had bought those, too. "Chamomile would be great," she said.

Paul made a cup of tea for her and hot chocolate for himself.

"You want to talk," he said, coming out of the kitchen with

matching glazed coffee mugs he had bought one day when she took him to Cost Plus.

Shaundra took the mug from his hand. She had told Paul that chamomile was a relaxation tea, but that was no reason for him to add three tea bags to one cup. "I'm okay, I guess. I don't even know where to start. Things are bad. Real, real bad."

She blew over the mug and sipped. Her face twisted a little. "I put in a little brandy, lemon, and honey. Figured you needed something extra."

"Thanks," she said, and she sipped again. Shaundra had real issues with people making random decisions in her life. It took away her control. As long as she was in control, she felt okay. "Did you add the extra ingredients and the extra tea bags because I scared you at the house?" She sipped, but glanced at him in the corner of her eye.

"Woman, please." He kept stirring his cocoa. "You think I ain't ever experienced a mad black woman?"

The expression on his face almost made Shaun want to smile, but she didn't have the energy. "So you pick 'em crazy, I gather."

"Shit, if a woman ain't got a little fire, I don't want nothing to do with her. Least you know where you stand with fire—you're gonna get burned eventually. But with them holier than holy, docile, medicated-seeming gals, shit, you don't know what to expect." He raised a spoonful of cocoa to his lips. "This is some good shit."

Shaundra nodded, falling back into her daze.

Paul put his cup down and took hers from her hand. "Come here," he said.

The contact was more than she could handle at this point. Touching broke down her tough-black-woman exterior.

"What's going on, Shaundra?" Paul asked, her face upon his thin chest.

"I'm losing my family. That's what's happening."

"You can't lose your family, Shaundra. Your family is always yours, like it or not."

"Yes you can." Shaundra wiped her eyes on the purple throw. "It's happened to me before."

Paul hesitated for a moment, not sure if he should make her unearth the places she had come from. "Don't talk about nothing you don't feel like talking about, Shaundra. Stuff has happened to me that I don't ever intend to talk about as long as I am skinny and black."

"My mom. I lost her. And I will never get her back, no matter how hard I try."

"I thought you told me your mother was alive."

Shaundra adjusted the blanket around her shoulders. "She is. Lives about ten minutes from me, but she may as well live on a different planet. She left us. Bought us some groceries, then she left saying that she would be back in a couple of weeks. How do you leave a twelve-year-old and a fifteen-year-old in an apartment by themselves?"

"I don't know," Paul answered, and began to rub her back.

"I don't either. That's why I've always tried to be a strong mother to Brandi, and I have never put a man before my child, not even when I was married. I went through that; I wasn't going to do it to my daughter."

Paul kept rubbing. "Is that why you're mad at your mother?"

Shaundra felt tears coming on, but they were angry tears. "I'm not mad at her. She was weak. You can't expect someone who is weak to protect you. It ain't gonna happen. I'm mad at myself because I feel like I just did the same thing to Niecee that our mother did to us—I stopped having her back and left her without protection."

"Hold up, Shaun. Your sister is a grown woman. If she disrespects your house and lets your daughter have men over in the middle of the night, it's your duty to put her out."

Shaundra could hear the military in him coming out. "It's not that easy."

"I didn't say it was going to be easy, but your daughter is supposed to be your first priority. I would straight snatch my kids away from Lydia if I thought she was putting anybody before my kids."

Shaundra pushed up off his chest.

"I do put her first. I just—" Shaundra slapped her knees. "You just don't understand. Niecee saved me." A look of concern spread over her forehead.

"Don't torture yourself. You can't let something somebody did for you back in the day hang over your head."

"It's not that easy."

"Why not?"

She felt trapped. She wanted to tell him. She'd never told anyone, but she wanted to tell *him*. It was getting too heavy for her. She tried to prepare herself.

Shaundra took a deep breath and held the lukewarm mug of chamomile between her hands to steady herself.

"My mom left to go find my stepfather. I mean, he wasn't even my stepfather at the time. He was her longtime boyfriend and they broke up because he couldn't handle the weight of leaving his three kids back in Mississippi. She handled it at first. But then she didn't. I was twelve, but even then, it seemed she had given something to him she needed to keep for herself." Shaundra breathed hard again. "So my mother, a woman who needed to clothe and take care of her own two kids, quit her job at the nursery and curled into a ball for three weeks. When she came out of it, she went to Stater Bros., came back with five bags of groceries, and told us to hold tight, she'd be back in two weeks."

Shaundra was starting to feel lighter, but the hardest part was still ahead of her.

"So she left. Niecee made sure I got off to school and I ate, and at night she slept with me in my bed instead of in her own. She was there for me."

Paul grabbed his cocoa. "That's good, Shaundra, but you don't owe her for that."

Shaundra placed her hands out to stop him. "Just listen, Paul.

So she wasn't just gone for two weeks. And on the first, the rent was due, and we didn't have any money to pay it, of course—we were kids. When the owner of the building knocked on our door, we told him that our mother would be back any day and that she would take care of it as soon as she came home."

Shaundra started to cry. Not breakdown tears, but controlled tears that streamed at steady intervals.

"He didn't listen. Mr. Otis put a three-day-pay-or-quit notice on our door the next day. I was petrified. I kept telling Niecee, 'He's gonna kick us out and we're going to be homeless.' Niecee wouldn't cry. She would just tell me that she was going to handle it and for me not to flip out.

"Then all of a sudden it seemed like the situation changed. Mr. Otis seemed cool. The pressure was off. He didn't put any more notices on our door. I asked Niecee what she did and she just told me that she worked out an arrangement; she just had to do some odds and ends for him after school every day. I felt relieved and excited; we weren't going to get kicked out.

"I remember hugging her so hard. She didn't smile or anything. She didn't even hug me back. I asked her if she wanted me to help—I could pick up trash and stuff around the complex, water the grass. She told me when I got home from school to go straight in the house and to stay there. If anyone knocked, I wasn't to answer, and if Mr. Otis tried to talk to me alone, that I should just run. It wasn't until the next weekend that I caught on. Since his wife didn't work on weekends, Niecee had to do her odds and ends work in our own apartment. He knocked on our door; she answered and led him to our mother's bedroom. I just remember sitting in the closet behind the dirty clothes hamper hearing grown-up noises coming through the wall. The same noises that my mother made with our soon-to-be stepfather she had gone to Mississippi to retrieve.

"But really, Paul, when I think back, I don't think I ever heard Niecee make my mother's sounds at all. I only heard Mr. Otis grunting and talking about how pretty her long hair was. It was almost like he was doing it alone." Shaundra shook her head. "But he wasn't doing it alone. Because Niecee was locked in the room with him."

Shaundra looked Paul in the eyes and he looked back at her. Shaundra could feel he wanted to reach out to her but was afraid to, and at the same time, she wasn't sure she wanted to be touched.

"I always knew what happened, but we never talked about it. Niecee just went back to sleeping in her own bed instead of with me at night and spending a lot of time locked up in the bathroom by herself. She never complained or was mean to me. And when my mother came back, and my stepdad moved back in, everything seemed to go back to normal. But I know she saved me. I know it. Because whenever that man looked at me, I felt something I wasn't supposed to feel."

Shaundra had never seen Paul angry, but she knew what she was looking at. He balled his fist into his legs, and she could see his veins pulsing. "That was a nasty bastard. A nasty sick bastard."

Her tea was cold. She took a sip to clear the rancid taste in her throat. There was nothing left for her to say. And there was nothing she could hear that could make it all better.

22

As much as she wanted to be desired, the eyes made her feel uncomfortable. She'd always heard that the eyes were the key to the soul; she even believed it. But when she looked into the eyes of her soon-to-be customers, all she saw was drunken lust. The women were pretty much on their own in the club; this was evident by the six or seven hands that squeezed or brushed her behind on the way to the bar.

Maybe she didn't need one, but Brenda had to admit to herself that she wanted another one. Just enough to calm her nerves a little more and take the edge off.

"May I have a vodka and pineapple juice please?"

Edward handed a man his drink. "Eight dollars. Catwoman, I thought you didn't drink."

"I didn't." She crossed her arms over her halter.

Edward handed the man his change. "Smirnoff, Absolut, or Stoli?"

Brenda giggled, the high from her last drink taking effect.

He shook his head. "This one is on me. But don't get used to this shit. I ain't no charity worker."

Brenda shook her finger at him playfully. She had already given the DJ her playlist. If things went according to plan, she was up after KitKat, which meant she needed to be backstage before the end of KitKat's last song. The bartender handed her the drink. Sparkle, the young girl who had given her the vodka in the Styrofoam cup, was currently up. Brenda sipped her drink and watched how Sparkle worked the pole and the audience with ease. Talking to her in the pit, Brenda had gotten the idea that she hated her job, but watching her onstage, Brenda saw something completely different. The men loved her. Some whooped and hollered, others sat with their mouths suspended open.

The intensity in her eyes and expression was amazing. If Brenda didn't know better, she would think that Sparkle loved what she did and would never want to do anything different.

The vodka was just now starting to hit her spine. If Brenda had been hanging out with Shay, Shaundra, and Karina, this would normally be the part where she'd already be knocked out on the love seat after barely finishing one full drink. But Brenda would do as Sparkle said; she would let the alcohol kick in and just get on the stage and do her thing.

As Sparkle finished her performance and collected the stray dollars, the DJ announced that gentlemen could get special time with Sparkle in the VIP suite, first come, first served. No one had mentioned *special time* to Brenda in explaining the ropes. KitKat took the stage, and with drink in hand, Brenda made her way to the back. She wondered if she would have to give special time, and what special time consisted of. Sparkle was still backstage toweling off. Brenda walked over to her, trying to get her head off loaded status and back to normal.

"What's special time in the VIP room?" Brenda enunciated strongly, trying to make sure no slurring made it through her radar.

"It's premium time, girl. Three songs for a hundred dollars."

"Three dances?"

Sparkle held her money in one hand, then draped her bikini top around her neck as she toweled off her breasts. "Yeah, girl, you get two or three of those in a night and you go home with a nice piece of change. That's where the money is. I gotta go. Time to service my men."

By the middle of KitKat's second song, Brenda wanted to feel nervous, but she didn't. There was a superficial film of warmth all over her body. All the other strippers had chosen bootylicious-rumpshaker kind of songs. Brenda decided to come with a different slant. Though she had reasonably mastered the booty clap, rump-shaking wasn't her forte. As KitKat exited the stage, Brenda heard her name being announced.

"Next up, on her first time to the stage is Mardi Gras. Y'all get ready for her to pop that coochie on you Brazilian style. *Mardi Gras!*"

Brenda heard a loose round of applause. She breathed in. As soon as she heard her first song, Missy Elliott's "Pussycat," she reached out for the curtain.

When she stepped onto the stage, all eyes were on her. Everyone looked expectant. Brenda rolled her body and rubbed her hands over her breasts. She heard a small "Whew" come from somewhere in the back of the club. She jiggled her breasts, and the next "Whew" was longer. She wanted to smile, but didn't. Brenda stepped farther onto the linoleum-covered stage. She eyed the men sitting around the stage, then licked her lips—slowly, so that her tongue left a trail of wetness across her lips. Someone said, "Mardi Gras." *Mardi Gras*—that was the closest thing to a cheer she had ever gotten in her life. She felt something click on inside of herself. She did like this. She did want this. As she danced, she focused on how desired she felt. A man walked up to the front of the stage and offered her her first dollar. She moved in waves over to him and reached down with her hand. "No, your G-string," he said. Despite the height of the heels, Brenda managed to squat down. The man, who happened to be a little chubby, but fairly handsome, slid the dollar under the blue sequined strap showing above her skirt. The man seated next to him did the same. How could Sparkle say that stripping was hard on a sistah? Stripping was the closest thing to true desire she had ever felt.

Once the first song was over, Brenda knew the second song would be harder; she would have to show her body on this one. The music started. Brenda closed her eyes and tried to concentrate on her choreography.

*Baby, the lights are low and I'm right outside your door. Do
you want me . . .*

Brenda rolled her neck back and scratched all ten of her fingers down her oiled neck, down her breasts, onto her stomach.

*You already know what I came here for.
I want to feel you, ohhh.*

With both hands on her stomach, she thrust her pelvis back and forth in quick, snapping motions that made it look like she was in the middle of a convulsion. She rolled her neck back again.

I'll strip before I enter. No need to undress me tonight . . .

Mid–neck roll, she pulled the bottom strings from her halter. It hung loosely over her breasts.

I'm on a mission to make your body shiver. I have all you need between these sweet thighs.

She untied the top strings.

My heels are off; my hair is down. I know your girlfriend is out of town. I got you, boo.

She strung the blue, yellow, and red sequined halter between her breasts, then dropped it to the ground.

The crowd went wild. Brenda cupped her bare breasts and bit her bottom lip. She watched the dollars waving, but she didn't jump at them. They would have to wait.

Let me start with your toes. I'll worship you from the ground up.

Brenda unsnapped the skirt. It fell to the ground. Brenda licked her right middle and index fingers, then slid them down her body until her fingers met her crotch.

I'm delicious. My mouth will melt all your fears away. I'm your freak. I'll do all you need me to.

She put her two fingers under the band of her thong. Her fingers touched her flesh. It was wet.

Is the sky what you want? I'll take you there. I'm yours to ride. I want you inside me tonight.

With her fingers still inside her crotch, she turned her behind toward the audience and bent her upper body toward the linoleum. She flashed a quick glimpse of her vagina. The bill-holding hands reached out toward her.

Baby, on your back now . . .

Brenda dropped to her knees and rolled over onto her back. Her legs pointed straight up into the air. She rolled her back on the ground and inch by inch let her legs part into a wide V.

Your body looks tasty. I'll sit on you slowly. Receive your passion into me.

She massaged the inside of her legs, then let her legs drop from a V into a full split with her toes touching the floor from her glass-bottomed shoes. She rubbed her twat, then popped her vagina hard with her left hand like she was spanking it.

"Mardi Gras!" was yelled from so many spots in the audience, Brenda didn't know which way to look first.

Do you want me?

Brenda was ready. She squeezed her breasts between both of her arms and started to raise herself up. She bent her torso forward and dropped it down between her legs. She crawled on her belly toward the edge of the stage.

My heels are off; my hair is down. I know your girlfriend is out of town. I got you, boo.

A man put a twenty-dollar bill into her mouth. Brenda bit down on it.

Remember, I'll take you to the sky. I'm yours to ride.

She ended by humping the ground, her nipples touching the linoleum lightly, then breaking contact. Lightly, then breaking contact.

I'll worship you . . .

"Whoooooooo!" broke out around the club. Brenda smiled. She smiled big and brazenly. She was proud of herself. "I actually went through with it," she mouthed to herself. As the crowd applauded, Brenda stayed on her knees collecting all of the money that had been thrown her way. There were a lot of dollar bills, but there were quite a few fives and a couple of tens.

"Let's hear it for Mardi Gras," the DJ said from his booth. "If you want to spend some special time with Mardi Gras, head back to the VIP room and she will take care of you. Remember, this is virgin ass. If you want to be her first, make your move quick."

Brenda didn't know what to expect from the lap dances. The couple she'd seen in the club had taught her that they were always done topless. As she stepped down the three steps from the stage, she thought about the lap dance she had gotten from Mackie at the other club.

"Hold up, honey, you need to count out."

"Sorry," Brenda said, staring at the short woman in her late forties who didn't look like she was taking shit from anyone. The woman rolled her eyes. Brenda handed the woman her money.

The bills moved quickly in the woman's hand. "Twenty, forty, seventy, eighty-five." She counted the bills again, then placed Brenda's numbers in her book. "Put it in your locker or wherever. When you come out of VIP, any money you come out with is new money. It will be added on to this. So don't be stupid. Sign here."

Brenda still felt a little loopy, like she still needed to watch her speech. "Would you keep it?"

The woman looked at her crazy, like she'd just asked to borrow a thousand dollars. "I ain't your momma. You need to handle it. I got too many girls to hold money."

Brenda rolled the money up in her hand. "Thanks."

"You better not be gettin' smart. Get back to VIP before you miss your spot."

23

I dressed. It felt like I was going to a funeral, yet at the same time, I was happy to be going. Two hours before I got out of bed, and most of the evening before, I had thought about what I was going to wear.

It was Sunday. Marcus had already left for church. I got up and leafed through my closet one more time. I wanted to be sexy but sensible. I wanted him to know I dressed especially for him, but I didn't want him to feel too special. I decided on a pair of fitted jeans, a red, ribbed mock turtleneck, a black belt, and black leather boots.

Maybe I am lying to myself by saying that I wanted to feel like Marcus's wife this particular day. I had on my wedding ring and I woke up in our bed, but when I dressed, I dressed for Darius. The soap I used was for Darius, the way I plucked my eyebrows, the way I had gotten the front half of my braids redone the day before, my perfume . . . all for Darius. I hadn't ever cheated on Marcus, except for my daily masturbations, and with or without the rules my mother-in-law had laid out for me before I married her son, I wasn't quite sure that was cheating at all. Maybe it was. I lent my body to strange and familiar men. I wanted their bodies on top of mine, even on Sunday. But these men were just in my head. Darius was real.

I had never visited anyone in prison. When Darius first started making trips to juvenile hall, I decided I never would. I told myself that he had abandoned me and that I didn't care if he rotted in there. Eventually, he would get out and Shaundra would tell me she saw him driving his mother's car or she ran into him at the concession stand at the movies. I was already married to Marcus and I pretended not to care. I called him a punk-ass and a no-good trifling-ass Negro. But the bottom line remained. I still loved him.

After I finished dressing, I found it hard to eat breakfast. Usually I hounded down some French toast dips from the freezer or a big bowl of cornflakes with thick chunks of banana. All I could do today was drink a little coffee and eat half of a peeled orange. I wanted to look good for him. I didn't want to feel bloated. I was nervous.

I sat in the prison parking lot almost the same amount of time I actually visited with Darius. The lot was filled with cars. The dullness of the rain matched the drabness of gray buildings that towered to the front and side of me. Something seemed permanent about these buildings, like once I went in, a part of me was never going to be able to get out.

The first building I went into looked like a normal building from the inside except for the metal detectors. It almost felt like I was going to the courthouse to defend myself on a traffic ticket. But after I filled out the little form, gave my driver's license, and they inspected me and my Spartan belongings—keys, quarters in my front pocket, and a half-full bottle of water—every place I walked into from that point on was like walking deeper into hell. The worst part is the first time a gate closes behind you. The noise rings in your head, and even when you manage to forget it, eventually the sound comes back. The second worst part is the smell. Nothing looks out of place, everything looks basically clean, but as soon as your nose catches on, you realize that it's ripened flesh you are smelling. Flesh is something prison has more than enough of.

I got to the visiting room before Darius did. There were two guards and two cameras that I noticed right off. The room itself was large, with a soda machine and another machine with chips and candy against one wall. The chairs and the tables were sturdy but small—I imagined so that people couldn't pass things under the table. Smart thinking, I guess. The pamphlet had said that I could bring five dollars in quarters for the machines; I did, but I had never put that much money in one vending machine at a time.

At first the room seemed impersonal. All the inmates, loved ones, and histories in one space without any walls separating us. I felt commingled. Like I was a part of everything happening in that room. But when Darius entered, my world got small again. He shrunk me back down to size.

He touched me on my shoulder first, from behind. I wondered how he knew it was me, with the braids and all; I'd also gained a little weight since the last year we'd seen each other. I stood up. Then I turned around.

There were no words for this. Darius looked me in the eye; I looked up to him, he hugged me so that my lips rested against his neck, and then he kissed me. Just lips, no tongue. I shuttered.

"Shay, girl," was the first thing out of his mouth.

"Darius," I said.

The pamphlet had said that only brief contact was allowed at the beginning and the end of each visit. I wanted to touch him. I wanted to be up under him. I wanted conjugal visits. I sat my insane ass down.

"You look good," I told him. He sat down.

"You look better than I remember, but about the same. I mean . . ." He leaned forward and let his hands fall between his legs.

I just wanted to smell him.

"You looked like I'da thought you'd look," he continued. "You know, since a niggah ain't seen you in so long, I had to imagine that your hips were fuller, your breasts. That your hairstyle woulda changed to something current. A niggah's present can't be his past, right? So I update you every day. In my mind you change little by little, but I notice every change."

Darius was in mack mode and I knew it. His mackaliciousness

had always worked on me, though. Something about it came from a sincere place.

In my own imagination, I hadn't done as good a job as he had. Whenever I envisioned him, I always saw the young Darius. The last Darius I had seen in the flesh, the one with the boyish face. In my fantasies, the only thing that had grown on him was his dick. I laughed, but only on the inside.

The Darius that sat in front of me looked like a fully grown man. His head was bald, the color of perfectly browned bacon. *I always loved bacon*, I thought to myself. His arms were gigantic, and had I been able to burn a hole through his jumpsuit, I knew his chest was off the chain.

It shouldn't have, but for me, emotionally, it felt like the first day after his first arrest. I just wanted to kiss him and tell him everything was going to be okay—something I had never managed to say to him. I just moved on hook or crook. I had never thought of things this way. I looked down at my wedding ring. Maybe I had abandoned him.

"So what have you been up to?" I said, just to pull myself out of my mental rut.

"Hoping to see you. I'm a grown-ass man, and as grown as I am, you still got me whipped on you."

"Shut up, Darius," I said. I would have slapped his leg, but I didn't think I was allowed to.

"See what I'm sayin'," he smiled. Why the fuck did he do that? His teeth were still so beautiful and white. Lickable. He continued, "Don't no girl talk to me crazy, but you. I let you handle me like I'm your be-otch. You the G girl."

I didn't know what to say to Darius. I wanted to bring up Rita—did she get his ass sprung too?—but I decided not to be trifling. Rita was none of my business. Neither was little Darius.

"Whatchu got your mind on?" Darius asked.

"Nothing," I said. "You want something from the vending machine? I brought a shitload of quarters."

"Let's roll." Darius stood up next to me and we walked over to the far wall. Walking to the vending machine felt like a date. We walked closely, so close, I imagine if I would have closed my eyes and concentrated, I would have felt his energy meeting mine.

"My treat," I said.

"Ladies first," he said. "The damn Cheetos are bangin' in here."

"Cheetos it is. And what, do you think I should go old-school and get an Orange Crush?"

Darius flashed a quick lightning smile. "You ain't changed."

"I know," I said. I had changed. If I was out of the house and not with Marcus, a margarita would replace a soda any day of the week.

"What you gettin'?"

Darius cracked his knuckles. "Oh, you know your boy. Straight up Twix, baby, and Coke all the way."

"Your ass ain't changed," I said, resisting the urge to touch him again.

He smiled. "I know what I'd like to be eatin' and drinkin'."

I didn't look at Darius as I put the change in the machine. I knew what I wanted to be eating and drinking as well.

Maybe this wasn't the greatest idea in the world. I had gone so many years without seeing Darius, why did I have to go and fuck up my program now? Being with him was taking me way back to high school. My speech was changing. My mannerisms. I hadn't had a damn Orange Crush since Darius's ass acted a fool and got caught. Every time I saw a can of it, I wanted to throw it upside his head. That was my personal mission: never to see Darius again and never, ever, again drink an Orange Crush. I was back-sliding with a quickness.

We sat back down at our table. The orange liquid felt good going down my throat, the way most sin feels the first time you do it. Darius offered me half of one of his Twix bars. I let him grab a few Cheetos from my bag.

"You're right, the Cheetos do taste better here," I said to him.

"You gonna have to come back then."

"Naw, I don't think I can do that."

"Shay." Darius touched my leg. I expected guards to rain down on us, but nothing happened. "Whatchu talkin' 'bout, girl? You ain't coming back? You've dissed me for over ten years; you can't be messin' with a niggah like that. I write you; you don't ever write me back. How the fuck am I even supposed to know you out there?"

"You know. The same way you know Rita and Little Darius are out there. Because they are." I felt a slight ghetto roll trying to take over my neck. I pointed my finger instead.

"Don't be putting yo' finger in my face, Shay. You know I don't like that shit."

I kept my right index finger out and inched it the tiniest bit closer to his face. "What if I come up here one day and they're here, then what? Oh, wait, because you only get three adult visitors per weekend, I would have to roll up here with her ass. Yeah, right."

Back in the day, Darius would have straight argued with me. He might have even shook me. As crazy as it sounds—and I would fuck a person up for touching me out of line—I wanted him to shake me. He was calm. Eventually he smiled.

"That's what this is really about, Shay. You just jealous cuz Rita got my son. It coulda been you."

My voice got low. I didn't want the guards to hear me acting out. "Yeah, niggah. It coulda been me cryin' all night because your ass got locked up again and again and again."

"Shut up, Shay."

"Naw, Darius, I'm on a roll. It coulda been me living with my momma, knowing to hell me and my momma don't even get along, just so I coulda had your baby and been able to have my welfare money stretch." I laughed. "Fuck, I coulda just lived with your momma so that way you wouldn't have to have your nappy-headed son bring your sorry-ass letters down to Shaundra's house. Yeah, it really coulda been me."

Darius tensed his fingers. His hands were so large, they scared me for a second. "Don't talk about my son, Shay. Dare's a good boy and he ain't did shit to you."

He was right, but it didn't stop my anger. I realized that some part of me thought that if I never saw Darius again, eventually all of my anger and hurt would go away. It just settled itself and waited. I breathed.

"He didn't do anything. You're right." Fuck, I couldn't believe it. I could feel the tears starting way in my stomach. I breathed again, but they didn't retreat; they just kept coming forward. "You know," I said speaking low, this time not because I didn't want the guards to hear me, but because I didn't want Darius to hear my voice crack. "Sometimes you think you grow up and you let shit go, but you don't. You hang on to it. When you move, you pack the shit up and you take it with you. I don't even know how to say this right, Darius, but prison, Orange Crush, and Little Darius have been my enemies for so long, I don't even know how to stop it anymore. You hurt me. You left me. Then you got her pregnant, the minute you got out."

Darius held his chin. He looked professor-like. Like he was about to break down a lesson for me that I didn't want to learn. He looked me in the eye. "When I got outta juvie, Shay, I woulda gotten any skeeza pregnant. Keena, Stacey, Renee Richards. It just happened to be Rita. She was the first one I connected with, and I went for mine. It wasn't about no love, Shay; it was about necessity. Think about it. When you need five dollars, you don't care who gives it to you. I needed a woman beside me; someone who wasn't gonna leave me when shit didn't work out right. Someone who was gonna have my back the *next time* I ended up in the joint. I knew I was gonna end up back on the inside. Niggahs always know. They just hope they get tired of doin' dirt before the police catch 'em dirty. I was going back and I knew that before I ever got out." Darius kept his eyes on me; it almost seemed like he didn't even blink. "So I needed a girl who was gonna have my back, just as fucked up as I managed to be on any given day, and that was Rita. That wasn't you, Shay. You showed me that when you married that trick-ass niggah and sent the invitation to my momma's house. That was some bitch-shit."

"You left me first, Darius."

"I ain't left you, Shay, I got locked up."

I flipped my braids out of my face. "No, Darius. You did some shit and got caught and they locked you up for what you did. You make it sound like shit wasn't your fault."

"You right, Shay. I did shit, I got caught, and you left."

I could see the hurt in Darius's eyes. I wondered if he could see the hurt in mine. I smashed the rest of the Cheetos left in my bag. "I didn't want this life, Darius. Just like you say you knew you were going to live it, maybe I knew it too and I didn't want to be dragged down with you. It's not fair. I've never loved anyone like I've loved you. Marcus, I love Marcus. But it is different, Darius. It's safe."

"It's safe, Shay, but you ain't happy. If you was happy, you couldn't have had that much excitement on yo' face when you first laid eyes on a niggah today. That was happy. I know what the fuck I'm talkin' 'bout."

I shook my head. As much as I hated disagreeing with Darius, I had to. "Happiness is not having to bring my child down to a prison to visit his father."

My comment didn't hurt Darius. He was resolved. "I'm 'bout to get out this piece, Shay. I ain't knowin' what I'ma do, but I ain't coming back up in here. What then? How are you gonna live with yourself knowing the niggah you really love is free and around the corner from yo' best friend's house?"

I didn't say anything. I just looked at him. The tears on my face were drying.

Darius smiled, but it was a cold smile. The kind, I imagined, you pick up in prison.

"Yo' face says everything, Shay-shay. You ain't done with me. We connected. Even after one of us leaves this earth, we still gonna be connected. You may as well just ride the flow." Darius smiled again. He had spoken his gospel to me and he was through with it. I heard everything he said, but I didn't have a response. At least not one I was willing to share.

Darius had won. I could see victory under his skin. It was in his calmness. I knew right then, it didn't matter if I ever came back. He would always know that I wanted to. And when he got out this time, he would come looking for me. The biggest part of me would be waiting for him.

24

Paul dropped Shaundra off at home the next morning just after eight. Niecee wasn't there. Neither was Brandi. In any other circumstance like this, Shaundra would have wanted to cry or explode. But not now. She was calmed by total exhaustion and understanding.

Shaundra had let Niecee wreak havoc on her life because havoc had been wreaked on hers. That's why she had allowed the craziness with the ex-boyfriends. That's why she had allowed the weed smoking and late-night men who used to creep in and out of her doors before she'd put her foot down.

But things had changed now. Brandi was older, and she was paying attention to everything that happened in that house. She wasn't a little girl anymore; Shaundra had to run things accordingly. Paul wasn't going to be able to spend the night anymore when Brandi was home. When he did come over, he needed to leave by ten P.M., and when Shaundra went on dates, she would need to return by midnight. Lastly, she would spend the night at Paul's only when Brandi's good-for-little father had her or when she had another responsible adult to watch her.

Shaundra put away the things from her overnight bag, and began to take inventory of the house. Niecee's room looked ransacked. Empty hangers lay on the floor. Stray pieces of clothing trailed between the closet and the bed. Lipsticks, perfumes, and personal hygiene items lay across the bed. Everything looked picked through. Shaundra knew that Niecee had taken only her most important and necessary items with her and left the excess. Shaundra placed all the hangers and clothes on top of all the other stuff on the bed and walked across the hall to check out Brandi's room. The door was locked.

"Damn it, Brandi," Shaundra said aloud. She retrieved her keys from her dresser and unlocked the door. She thought about it. Maybe she should have been glad that Brandi locked the door; it showed that she still felt ownership and that she might be coming back.

"*Might be coming back?*" Shaundra thought to herself. She had never imagined she'd be going through this; she thought only white parents and bad mothers went through this type of thing. Right off, Shaundra noticed that Brandi had taken her schoolbooks. That was a good sign, she thought. The room wasn't ransacked, but something was definitely different. Little things were missing. Two pairs of jeans, a blue knit sweater, a couple pairs of tennis shoes. Shaundra looked on her daughter's study desk and saw that Brandi had left a bottle of black fingernail polish open and it had spilled and dried on the desktop. Shaundra shook her head and went to her own bathroom to grab a rag and nail polish remover. How could Brandi have wasted polish and left it on the desk to dry? Why would she want to wear *black* polish anyway? Shaundra sat down at Brandi's desk and began to clean.

She had bought this desk for Brandi when she'd turned thirteen. She figured that her daughter would want her own place to study and to put her stationery and schoolwork in. Niecee and Shaundra had never had that. There was no way on God's green earth that their mother would have spent four hundred dollars on a desk. Please. They had always done their homework at the kitchen or living room table. Shaundra had had so many hopes for Brandi. She still did, she guessed. "I don't know what's wrong with her," Shaundra said, as she put elbow grease into removing the black polish. The antique white finish on the desk was ruined. The polish remover had eaten into the paint to remove the polish. Before getting up, it had occurred to Shaundra to look through her daughter's desk, to see what else she could find that she didn't know about. She decided against it. At least at this point, she had already absorbed so much devastation.

She had already checked the bedrooms; now she checked the kitchen and both bathrooms. There was no note. She could feel the anger rising, but she tried with everything in her to push it down. Shaundra strolled into the kitchen and decided to make herself a midmorning drink. A dirty martini sounded good. She would drink her martini and wait. There was no way she could go to work today anyway; she was capable of hurting someone today. She would wait. Eventually something would happen.

25

Brenda put the eighty-five dollars in her locker, then wiped down her face, sweaty body, and feather mask. She was happy that it didn't fall off during either routine, though some feathers had gotten crumpled from her turning her head side to side on the linoleum. She stopped to stare at herself in the mirror ever so briefly. She couldn't help letting a smile spread on her face. The men had loved her, but the best part was that she loved it herself. She was still a little high from the alcohol, but this was something else she was feeling. She had been seamless. She had executed perfection and she felt it deep on the inside of herself. *This is what power feels like,* she thought. Men from the back of the room had come all the way up to the stage just to give her their money. It almost didn't make sense to her, how irrational they seemed, almost like giving her a few bucks gave them a piece of her. But as a woman, a woman who had never gotten much attention from men, a woman who had always faded into the background around her girlfriends, she had finally experienced a piece of the limelight, and she was grateful.

The VIP room was in the back of the club. It had smoked glass doors that couldn't be seen through from either side. She had expected a little room, like the one she'd gotten her first lap dance in, but this room was parceled off into four little nooks so that each client or group of clients was afforded a certain amount of privacy. Brenda hadn't see any of the small private rooms in the club yet, but she imagined in terms of ambience, this room was as good as it was going to get. *I've made it to the big time,* she thought to herself, and laughed.

"There's a guy waiting for you," the bouncer said from the

club side of the smoked glass. "His three songs don't start until the beginning of the next song. But you can start dancing and give him a little extra. Remember to collect the money: a hundred dollars, plus whatever he gives you as a tip."

Brenda nodded, and he opened the door for her. The first thing Brenda saw was a handsome black man sitting in a nook under a brass 2. In section 3, she saw Sparkle. She was completely nude, except for the orange G-string that was barely on her ass. She sat with her legs open on the gentleman's lap, her legs straddling his. One of his hands was on her breast and one was on her crotch. Brenda walked down the steps and over to her section, all the while keeping her eyes on Sparkle. When Sparkle noticed Brenda's stare, she made eye contact for a long second, then looked away.

"Hi, I'm Bren— Mardi Gras," Brenda said to the man in her section. Below the brass number 2 was a small printed sign that said: "Customers will be asked to leave the club for making indecent contact. Absolutely no hands on the strippers." Brenda was learning quickly that most of the real rules in this place were unwritten.

The man nodded to her, then took inventory of her from top to bottom. It occurred to her to say something like, "You like what you see?" But she didn't. She stood there, knowing that she should at least get closer to him. She thought about how during her first lap dance, the stripper had come in and completely taken control.

"So this is your first time?" the man said, still staring at her breasts.

"Yes," Brenda said, looking at his preoccupied eyes.

"Come here."

Brenda walked over to him. When she tried to sit to the side of him, he positioned her square on his lap.

"Just relax," the man said into her ear. "Just close your eyes."

Brenda did as she was told. The man kissed her ear, then

licked a trail down her neck. Brenda pretended not to feel it.

"You taste good," he said.

In her head, she was supposed to say, "You ain't tasted nothing yet," but she didn't. "Thank you," she said.

He repositioned her again so that she was sitting squarely on his penis. He held on to her hips and pushed them backward and forward. Brenda caught on and began to move her hips in tight circles.

"That feels good," he said.

As strange and unnatural as this situation felt, the verbal affirmation was assuring. Brenda sped up her circles. The man placed his hands back on her hips and directed her to slow down. He wanted deep, slow, grinding ovals.

As Brenda got into her groove, Sparkle walked past holding the hand of her gentleman customer. Had Brenda had her wits completely about her, she would have noticed that the man had to have been at least thirty years older than Sparkle, but she didn't. All Brenda thought about was that as soon as Sparkle walked out of the room, she was going to be alone with him.

Brenda concentrated on her ovals, while her customer untied the top and bottom strings of her halter.

"Do you like your breasts?" he asked in her other ear.

"Yes," she said, lying.

"They're perfect," he whispered. "They'd fit nicely in my mouth."

Brenda couldn't think of any response for that. She watched as the halter slid from her lap onto the carpeted floor.

"Oh, yeah," the man said. He squeezed both breasts simultaneously, then bit deeply into the right side of her neck.

A slight moan escaped from her mouth.

That must have been his signal, because he leaned his body back on the sectional, so that his penis felt longer and harder against her. He leaned her back onto him.

"Do you like this?"

Brenda nodded yes, thinking that was what she was supposed to do.

The man put his middle and index finger between her legs, on the outside of her blue sequined thong.

A squeal made it through her pursed lips. He massaged. Her clitoris felt full, and a warmth shot over her body that was stronger than the feeling of any alcohol. Brenda started to want him back, and it scared her. She hadn't been touched by a man like that in such a long time. She wanted to feel his hands all over her. At the same time, she didn't even know him.

"Will you take off your mask?"

Brenda shook her head somewhere between yes and no.

He reached for her mask, but she pulled his hand back down to her breast.

He shaped his hand around her breast and pinched her nipple just hard enough.

Brenda let out another moan. No man had ever done that to her before. He held her breast and kept his left hand circling her clit. Though her vagina was still covered, his aggressive touch made the material feel spiderweb thin.

"Does this feel good?" he asked.

"Yes," she said.

"Will you come with me?"

Brenda nodded and braced both of her arms around his neck. He pressed her down deeply on top of him. As she pulled, he pressed. Their bodies took over the moment. She felt a writhing in her pelvis that defied up and down or round and round. His fingers were glued to her clit. She let out a moan, this one more jagged than the ones that came earlier. Before she knew it, she felt a flood between her legs. She let her arms loosen from around his neck. He pressed her down on him again, then once more, and then she felt a stickiness on her behind that flowed through the crotch of his pants.

"Thanks, that was good," he said.

"You're welcome," she said back, avoiding his eyes.

Brenda didn't know how to feel afterward. She sat on the bench in front of her locker, toweling off. The touches had gone from feeling strange to good, but then, after she'd climaxed, she had started to feel unclean. She played the situation over and over again in her head. How desperate could she really be, she thought to herself.

"How'd it go?" Sparkle said, walking back into the pit.

"Okay." Brenda looked up; she noticed that Sparkle had changed into a gold metallic bikini.

"Did you bring any Vaseline or oil?"

"Vaseline." Brenda reached into her bag and handed her the jar.

"I guess this is big enough." Sparkle plopped her leg up on the bench and set the jar down next to her foot. "Plain baby oil works a lot better, and it doesn't stick to the man's clothes or the floor."

"Oh," Brenda said distractedly.

"Girl, what's up with you? Was something wrong with the guy?"

Brenda sat there. "I don't think anything was wrong with him. I think he did the same things any other customer would have done. I think he would have done the same thing with any other stripper. He came." Brenda looked up at her. She wanted to tell her that she had come too, but she was too embarrassed.

Sparkle switched legs. "Listen, in this business, if a man don't come after paying you a hundred dollars for three songs, you may as well hang your career up. That's what they come here for."

"Sounds like he may as well just go to a prostitute then."

Sparkle laughed and put her other leg down. "You know what?" She leaned down toward Brenda. "Best thing you can do is realize to that man, no matter how good, or sweet, or wholesome you are, you are a prostitute. Only difference is that you are a legal one. It's like the difference between alcohol and marijuana. They're both drugs, only one you can go to jail for. I'm about to get back to the floor. The pockets are decent tonight."

Sparkle started walking out and Brenda stopped her.

"Does everyone have to do VIP, or could I just do my stage act and do privates every once in a while?"

Sparkle spoke low. "You can do whatever you want, but that sounds like a sure way to get fired. You may as well just do what you have to do to make your cash. VIP is the way you make real money around here. What did that guy give you for a tip?"

"Twenty."

"And how much did you make from the stage?"

"Eighty-five dollars."

"Okay, tip out your bouncer and the DJ and you are still walking out of here with a nice little piece of cash, not to even think about the fact that you have at least one more set on stage and more VIP action."

"I'm not doing VIP."

"Whatever." Sparkle rolled her eyes. "But you didn't come up in here to try to play the shy roll. Niggahs are gonna nut on you. That's the hard fact. Wipe your ass off and move on like the rest of us. There ain't no other private rooms here besides VIP, so better to do it for a C-note with a little privacy than a dub on the floor in front of everyone. But don't get it twisted. You gonna have to do everything everybody else gotta do. You'll probably be asked to give a lap dance on the floor before the end of the night. So take your hundred or your twenty and keep rollin'. I'm telling it to you like it is."

It took about twenty minutes for Brenda to make it back out to the floor. The club was more packed than it had been when she'd left VIP. She'd changed into a red bikini with a silver sequined wrap and accentuated the ensemble with red and silver Mardi Gras beads around her neck. A ten-dollar bill was visibly tucked into her bra.

As she headed toward the bar, men checked her out here and there, but she just smiled and kept pushing forward. She needed another drink, and she needed it bad. Bad enough to want to feel the delicate burn in her throat. This was all too much, so much more than she had expected.

"Can I buy you a drink?" Brenda heard from right behind her.

"No," she said, not turning around, but trying to keep a smile in her voice.

"Aw, come on now. You gonna get me all sprung, then let me down like that." He kissed her ear.

Brenda turned around abruptly to see who it was.

It was him. The man who had granted her her first non-self-initiated climax in over five years.

"You sure you don't want that drink?"

Just looking at him was hard enough. She didn't even know his name. "Sure," she said, taking a seat.

26

Darius took me from behind. He wasn't angry, I was. I reached my arm back to slap him. I knocked him in the face. He slapped me harder than I slapped him, first on my back and then across my ass. He wanted me to feel the pain he inflicted, then he wanted to balance the pain with pleasure. He grabbed me by the hips and pumped hard into me. My juices flowed at a rate that was unnatural. Each motion solicited more moisture and heat. I wanted to be angry. He was making me feel too good. My body was starting to give in and synchronize with his rhythms. I tried my best to kick him between the legs. He flipped me. Immediately I lunged forward and bit him in the face. I wasn't aiming for his face, but somehow, in the rock and roll of the moment, my teeth ended up there. He pinned my knees to the ground with his legs, then took both of my nipples in his mouth at the same time and bit.

"Darius, stop," I said. "I hate you."

"You can hate me after I fuck you," he said.

"I'm still not going to be yours, Darius."

"You can fuck the man in the moon and you'll still be mine. I own you." He thrust forward and I moved. He did it again. I moved again. "See, you are stuck on the tip of my dick and I plan to be hard forever."

I don't know why Darius made me so horny, but he did. And it was the full-grown Darius pleasuring me now, not the man-boy of yesteryear. My mind, body, and juices had adjusted themselves accordingly. I wanted him, more than I had ever wanted him. All in my mind, I could feel him settling on top of me. He'd switched up. Now he stuck his fingers into me. He loved doing his index and middle fingers, but his favorite was the thumb because of its width and the big knuckle. No matter how many times I begged him to stick his dick into me, he wouldn't. He just said, "You hate me, remember?" Then he spread my legs apart wider. Darius had me across his lap. Every time I begged, he'd push his thumb in slowly then pull it almost completely out and watch my body quake in the aftermath. I did hate him. But I needed his penis and he knew it. He toyed with me. And just when he thought I couldn't take anything more, he laid me face down on the floor, put my legs over his shoulders, and stood halfway up. I felt like a human wheelbarrow. My breasts pointed toward the ground. When he stood up completely, my body slid up his and my mouth ended up on his bare penis.

"Suck it," he said. "And if you bite it, I swear, I'll never fuck you again."

The thought of that scared me. I began to suck. I wrapped my arms around his legs and began to taste more of him. Just when it got good, just when I thought I could climax from sucking him off, I felt the warm invasion of his tongue on my pussy.

"Shiiit." My body convulsed. I let my middle finger fall away from my clit and lay there on the couch catching my breath. It had been four days since visiting him, and my vagina was almost raw. I had mind-fucked Darius so many times, it was starting to wear on my body. Peroxide, cotton, and Vaseline were becoming my intimate friends. Something about seeing him put me into overdrive. I usually masturbated once every day or so, especially when I felt frustrated with my life, but now I was hitting the clit every time I had a dream or any stray thought about him that aroused me. Just thinking about him eating a Twix bar was enough to turn me on. The juiciness of his lips. How he licked them and took the crumbs into his mouth.

I wondered if Darius was working triple duty like I was. It comforted me, the idea that I wasn't doing this alone. I wanted him to be consumed too. I wanted him to write me and let me know that he was getting blue balls, he needed to fuck me so bad.

What if he never writes me again? I found myself thinking. I made myself stop. A much better thought was what Darius could do with me, his mouth, and a Twix bar.

27

Shaundra wasn't a drunk, but she had done her part to increase the profits of Absolut and José Cuervo over the past week. She hadn't seen hide nor hair of Brandi in three days. She hadn't even talked to Shay, Brenda, or Karina. She didn't know exactly why, but she knew a lot of it had to do with her pride. Shay had told her that something would go wrong soon. She had said that it could have something to do with Brandi. "Why didn't I listen?" Shaundra said, beating herself up. She hadn't gone to work since Brandi left. She hadn't even bathed, and anyone who knew Shaundra knew she loved to be clean and smell good. She'd spoken to Paul a few times, but that was only because he was the only person who knew something was going on, and she didn't want him worrying about her.

She'd been sleeping on the living room couch for the last two nights, with the television constantly tuned to the news. As long as she didn't see Brandi on the local news, she maintained a certain level of peace. Her peace was starting to wear really thin. It is the hardest thing in the world to try to sleep when your child is missing, no matter how old the child is. Since Brenda worked for law enforcement, Shaundra thought about asking her to check into the situation. She didn't want to file a missing persons report. That seemed too permanent and real. Maybe the police force could just be on the lookout for her.

Shaundra sat up on the couch and ran her fingers over her head. Her fade was starting to feel scraggly; she usually edged it up every three or four days. She adjusted the dial on the lamp to the second setting. Warm amber light broke up the blue shadows from the television. Shaundra squinted and searched around herself on the couch. The cordless phone had gotten pushed down into the side. She dialed.

"Hello, Shay, you busy?"

"Just finishing up something on the computer. One second . . . One more second . . . Okay. What's up, girl?"

Shaundra ran her left hand over her face. She either had to come out and say it, or lie. "It's okay, I was just checking in. I haven't talked to you in a few days."

Shay turned away from the computer. "You better not hang up the phone." Shay held the cordless to her ear and bent over to grab her shoes from under the computer desk. Whatever it was, it was serious. Shaundra was at home at eight on Friday morning, and Shay could hear the slightest slur in her words. "Tell me or I'll be to your house in fifteen minutes—talk."

She barely had the energy to talk. "Brandi gone; she left with Niecee."

Shay felt the sistah-girl roll take over her neck. "What?"

"They left last night. We had a big blowup. I kicked Niecee out because she let Brandi have a boy in her room." Shaundra didn't have the energy to tell her the full truth.

"In her room? A boy?" Shay went to the hall closet for her jacket.

"Brandi's having sex, Shay. I don't know how long it's been. I don't even know her anymore. I thought I knew Niecee. I just . . ."

"Don't beat yourself up, Shaun. You are the best mother I know. Sometimes shit happens to the best of us."

"You told me this was going to happen, you told me, Shay. I didn't listen."

Shay grabbed her purse, then headed to the kitchen to get her keys from the hook. "Just sit tight. I'm on my way."

28

He is actually nice, Brenda said aloud as she drove to the club. It was her third week, and Bruce had been in the club to see her four times. Okay, maybe he wasn't just there to see her, but that's how it felt. Brenda didn't see herself as the type to take ownership of a man, especially since she'd never really had one who was just her own, but she did find herself wondering about him. She'd wonder how his day at work went and if he had a stable woman in his life. Even though she had just seen him two days ago, she wondered as she drove if he was going to come down to the club tonight.

He'd already spent over four hundred dollars on dances in VIP, and he'd bought her a drink every night. She felt courted, and she liked it. The first night they sat together at the bar, everything seemed awkward. Brenda had already toweled down and washed up her private place, but looking at him, even over a drink, caused a strange sensation between her legs. At first, she would glance around the club or look down into her drink, but eventually she found herself giving all of her attention to him. Part of it was because he liked touching her, her arms, her shoulders. He looked a little like her mother's grandfather had looked when he was young. His wavy black hair, which wasn't an S-curl, reminded Brenda of the old pictures that used to sit on her mother's mantel. If Brenda judged correctly, he had to be around six feet two. She was five-ten, but figuring out his exact height was a little difficult because all of their time together was measured sitting down. She was either dancing for him or they were drinking and talking.

Bruce—the only black man she'd ever known named Bruce— was a fireman. The first night she'd spoken to him, she found herself wanting to talk about the things in her own life that had led her to public service. When she told him that she had become a police officer a couple years after high school, he laughed. He laughed so hard he had to wait a second to take a sip of his drink.

"That's funny," he said. "You got jokes, girl."

At first it shocked her that the idea of her being an officer was so unbelievable to him. Then it disappointed her, but she quickly got over it. She had promised herself that she wasn't going to mention her personal life anyway. She could get in a lot of trouble. Brenda took a sip of her drink.

"Yeah, I'm just kidding." She smiled. "But I did take a class at the junior college to become a court reporter. I just never finished it."

"I like a girl who is good with her hands." That's all he said before he started talking about the rigors of living at the firehouse several days a week, crazy work schedules, and stress. Brenda pretended not to have a clue. She had switched paths. And as much as her new path opened her up to things she never would have experienced otherwise, it also closed other things out. She had to remember that she was a stripper to him and not a potential girlfriend.

He didn't make her feel like a stripper, though; she felt more like a woman he desired and couldn't get enough of. When she was with him, even though she barely knew him, she imagined she was his lady.

Brenda resisted the desire to look at herself in the rearview mirror. "You're a stripper," she said, thinking about how great the chemistry had been between them the night before. Her words mixed with the mellow Oleta Adams lyrics coming from the car stereo. She waved to D.W., one of the bouncers, as she entered the parking lot. She would go in tonight and do her job. She wasn't going to worry about Bruce and what she couldn't be to him. She wasn't going to wonder if he ever came in on her nights off and took dances from other women. She was simply going to be a stripper, and tonight she would do her job well.

29

There are times when you come into consciousness and you realize that you are completely out of control. It didn't take me long to realize that I had spiraled, but it did occur to me that I should have noticed the descent long before I did.

Marcus and I were in trouble. It was more than that, though. I was in trouble. It seemed like my very soul was on the verge of getting wiped out. I felt antsy. Being alone was a thing I used to love, but now I found it hard to sit still. If I started to write, my mind wandered. If I decided to cook, it took me twenty minutes just to narrow down my choices. Working my pole and thinking about Darius were the only two things that held my attention. It felt like every window in me was open and I wasn't enjoying the draft. I wasn't enjoying anything and I didn't know how to talk about it. I wanted to tell my friends, at least my best friend, Shaundra, but no words would come to me to articulate where I really was. I was lost, that's the only thing that kept looping through my mind. How do you tell somebody that you are at the bottom of yourself? If you're me, the sad thing is, you don't. Because no matter how much you are hurting, no matter how much you want to be loved and understood, your pride is more important. I didn't have anything else to stand behind.

I was disappointed in myself. Disappointed that I hadn't gotten to the point where my inside health was more important than the outside appearance. That was one of my biggest problems with Marcus: He always wanted to put the right perception on things, but now that the shit was hitting the fan, I realized I was more like him than I ever believed. I had never looked at it that way before now. I had been so mad at Marcus over the years because I couldn't do this or that because it wouldn't look right. Right down to him not wanting me to have an hourly job. If I didn't have a respectable career, I couldn't have anything. I laughed. The biggest part of me knew that he wouldn't find the idea of me writing sex tales acceptable. That was why I didn't tell him. I wouldn't tell him until I was good and ready, and maybe not even then.

I sat there at my computer doing nothing. It seemed to me that most folks marry the illusion of the person they are with, not who that person really is. Marcus had to have married the person he thought I would become. Looking at myself, I wasn't sure the reality of me was something he would like at all. I drank, I loved to punctuate my sentences with curse words, and I owned a stripper's pole that was right under our marriage bed.

I had to see. I wanted to know if Marcus could really accept me for who I really was. I wasn't a church girl. I was wild, and that was never going to change. I loved sex, but I had never managed to love it with him. I wanted to be whole, once and for all. So that's why I decided to dance for him on my pole. It worked for Shaundra and her man, maybe it would work for me. I figured at least he would see me for real. He would come face to face with my raunchy side and not be able to excuse it away. He would see the biggest part of me and not be able to put a church hat on it. I needed this. So did he. If Mark couldn't see who I was after I worked a pole for him, he would never see me. This was our crossroads. All I had to do now was time it.

30

Before Shay could get in the driveway good, Shaundra came running out of the house.

"Go," Shaundra said, jumping into the car.

"Where?" Shay said, already starting to back up.

"Left out of the subdivision, hurry up."

Shay passed Darius's mother's house and barely glanced. "Where are we heading?"

"Right, here. To Workman."

"The Workman District? They're in Workman?"

"Yeah, they're in a hotel next to some strip club. Tits and Ass on Stockton Street. Brandi said the sign is real big and they're at the hotel on the right. It doesn't have a marquee."

"You know that's the ho district. You know that, right, Shaundra? Niecee has Brandi in some ho motel."

"Left, Shay, here." Shaundra held on to the dashboard. She had a Pistons cap on her head, a green coat, and some beige slippers. "I'm trying to get to her as quick as I can to get her out of there. Left, Shay."

"She asked you to come pick her up?" Shay asked.

"No, she called me to tell me that she and Niecee needed two hundred more dollars to pay for the rest of the week."

"I don't care what you say, Shaundra, Niecee needs a good ass whippin'. A straight beatdown."

"I can't argue right now, Shay. I just need to get to my daughter."

"You're right. Does she know you're coming to get her?"

"Shay, no. Turn right." Shaundra's voice was tense. "You already asked me that. I told her I would bring her the money. She tried to get me to put it on my credit card—"

"Niecee's idea, no doubt."

Shaundra rolled her eyes. Shay was working her nerves. She just needed to see her daughter to know that everything was okay. "There it is. Turn left into the lot."

Before Shay stopped the truck completely, Shaundra was jumping out. "You want me to go up with you, Shaun?"

"Stay here, Shay. I'll be back," she said as she trailed away.

Shay turned off the engine but let the CD player stay on. She'd been in a Sade "Love Is Stronger Than Pride" kind of mood. She pressed the repeat button on the steering wheel.

The motel was nasty. It was a beige color with dirt lines crying down the front and side of it. The bright orange trim only made the rest of the building look worse. Shay glanced around. The positive thing was that the motel fit in with rest of its surroundings. Everything on the street was drab and tired. Even Tits and Ass, with the bright red sign in block letters, looked spent. Shay was fascinated. It was past eight-thirty in the morning and men were still leaving the club. A couple of prostitutes were posted out front to get the strippers' leftovers.

Shay glanced over to the motel then back to the club. In the adjoining lot, she saw a woman leaving the club who strongly resembled Brenda from behind. She was with a man, but the man didn't look familiar. The woman had on black sweats and her hair was in a low-riding ponytail. She had to be about Brenda's height with the same type of build. Shay watched the girl walk the perimeter of the building, then disappear around the corner. Shay laughed. Yeah, right, Brenda at a strip club. She laughed again, and turned to watch a man checking the phone booth in front of the motel for change. Shay glanced back over at the lot. "Let it go, Shay," she said to herself. Besides, that girl worked there, as evidenced by the fancy headgear thing that covered her face.

After repeating "Keep looking" four times in a row, Shay was tempted to get out of the truck. Shaundra could have walked into any situation; she should have at least allowed backup to accompany her in. Shay gave the motel the once-over again. As she tried to calculate how many rooms she thought were on the premises, she heard a knock on her window.

"You got some change?"

Shay checked the door lock. "No," she said, and shook her head.

"Come on, man, you got something in a ride like that. Give me some change, man." He placed his hand on the window.

Shay started the engine. "I ain't got no change. Get away from me before I run your ass over. I ain't playin'."

He checked her face before he walked off. Shay kept mad-dogging him as he walked away. Someone knocked on the other side of the truck. She jumped.

"Let me in," Shaundra said. Brandi was with her. Shay clicked the front and back doors unlocked.

"Hey, Brandi," Shay said.

Brandi didn't say anything. She put both of her bags on the backseat and jumped in.

Shaundra would normally step in to correct Brandi's inappropriate behavior toward adults, but she didn't this time.

"Thank you for driving, Shay" was all she said.

Shay took off, deciding not to say a word.

31

Whatever Bruce's problem was, Brenda wasn't going to worry about it. This was her first time working a Wednesday, and it was a slow night compared to Thursday through Sunday. She noticed him as soon as he walked into the club, though she didn't want her radar to be so sensitive to his presence. She pretended to ignore him. She didn't even look in his direction until he sat at a table with a shot of Old Granddad in his hand, just ten footsteps from where she was giving a lap dance to someone else on the floor.

Today was Brenda's peacock costume day. Instead of her saving up for a car as she had expected to do, most of her second income ended up going toward new costumes. This one had real peacock feathers covering the bikini top and bottom as well as the mask.

"Do you like that?" she said to the gentleman behind her.

He nodded as she worked her booty over his penis and ball sack.

"I like it. It makes me feel nasty," she said, untying the top strings of her bikini and letting the bikini hang. She massaged her own breasts, then got up to jiggle them in his face. He stuck out his tongue.

"Unh-unhh. No tasting. That's what the VIP room is for. It takes a lot more money to taste this. But you are so cute, I might . . ." She inched her breasts closer to him and stuck out her tongue. "No, I can't."

She was playing with him and he liked it. Every move she made, he watched it like it was the only move that mattered.

She hadn't thought she was talking too loudly, but clearly she had been or else Bruce was good at reading lips.

"Yeah, man, she's the shit in VIP. I always come hard. She's the only one of these hos I give my real money to." Bruce toasted his shot glass to the air toward her and smiled. "Great piece of ass."

Brenda's eyes were burning. It took everything in her not to fall apart. She hadn't seen Bruce in about a week and a half, and for the life of her, she couldn't figure out what she had done to him to make him say that, even if in his mind, it was true. She couldn't think about his intentions right now, though. She still had one set to do.

When the song was up, she kissed the customer lightly on the lips. "He's right, I'll make you feel real good. Otherwise this fool wouldn't be paying my house note every month." She was sure not to look at Bruce. The customer placed a twenty and a five-dollar bill in her thong. Brenda immediately went over to the counter behind the stage to count out.

After her set, Brenda toweled off and went over to VIP. Jason was the bouncer at the door. "Section 4," he said.

"Thanks," Brenda said, then looked around the club quickly to see if she noticed Bruce. He wasn't anywhere to be found. "Shit," she said, before walking in. She took a deep breath.

Just as she had thought, Bruce was sitting in section 4, the nook way in the back with the most privacy. Brenda started to say something but then decided against it. If she hadn't learned anything else from her five weeks stripping, she had learned this—she was just the legal kind of prostitute as far as most of the men were concerned. Sparkle had been right.

"I'll start when your first song starts," Brenda said, sitting on the last cushion of the booth and crossing her legs.

"Come on now, you didn't miss me? I don't get any extra time?"

She wanted to say "hell no" with all her heart. "No."

"Damn, I must have fallen off."

"I guess so," she retorted.

When his song started, Brenda removed her peacock-feathered top and left it on the far cushion. She straddled his body facing him. As she gyrated, her breasts rubbed against his sueded silk shirt. His penis was already hard; his fingers molded themselves around the small of her back.

"Does that feel good, baby?"

Bruce pushed her more deeply onto him. "Don't talk to me like you talk to the rest of your customers." He sucked one of her breasts into his mouth. Brenda was sure it was going to leave a mark, but the harshness of the sucking turned her on. Bruce switched to the other breast.

Brenda tried to stifle her moan. "You talk to me like I'm any other *HO* working here, so why should I treat you differently?"

Bruce pushed her down hard onto him again. This time he held her still and gyrated against her. "I haven't seen you in a week and a half. I knew if I made you mad, tonight would be almost as good as make-up sex. Besides, I was just jealous seeing you with that guy. You're my girl."

His words softened her. Only couples and people who had relationships had make-up sex, Brenda thought, and he called her his girl. He had been her first, and she had never given anyone else lap dances like the ones she gave him. He even knew the exact amount of time that had passed since he last saw her.

He kissed her neck, then held both sides of her face with both hands and brought her lips to his. With all of the fake rules in this establishment, one of the only things she had never seen a girl do was kiss a guy.

Bruce put his tongue in her mouth. She sucked it into her; he tasted like whiskey. He kissed her so hard, her moan was suffocated between their heated breaths. It felt so good to have a man's tongue in her mouth again.

"You make me feel good, Mardi; you make me feel so good." Brenda kept kissing him; he made her feel good too.

Bruce kept one hand on her neck and moved his other hand

into the space between his penis and her crotch. He placed his hand on her clitoris, and she shuddered. Bruce pulled her closer to him and took his middle and index finger and placed them inside her thong. For the first time, Brenda felt flesh on flesh, though every other time he had still made her climax.

"Bruce."

"Shhhh," he said. He pushed both of his fingers through her vaginal folds into her. "Your pussy is so wet. Ohhh, you feel so good. Tight." He pressed his fingers more deeply inside of her.

Brenda kissed him again. This time it was harder to control her squeals.

"Let me fuck you, Brenda; I need to feel my dick inside of you."

Brenda kept kissing him, but shook her head no.

"I have a condom on me right now. No one is in here. Nobody will know."

"I can't," Brenda said, her words caught between kiss and breath.

"Please, baby." He twisted his fingers inside of her and pulsed them double time.

He called her baby. Brenda started to quake.

He could feel the climax catching on the inside of her. "Please, tonight, after the club, after you get off. We don't have to do it here. We can go to my place, your place. Whatever. Just let me have you."

Brenda continued to kiss him. Her kisses said it all.

32

"Shay, sorry to wake you up."

My voice was rough. "Shaun, you are out of line." I glanced at the clock. "It's two o'clock in the morning."

"I know, I know," she whispered. "I just needed to ask you something. It can't wait."

"Who is that?" Marcus asked, waking up, his arm around my waist.

"Shaundra," I said, looking back at him. Marcus rolled his eyes. "Baby, it's important. I'll take it in the den. One second, Shaundra."

I grabbed my robe hanging from the edge of the headboard, and didn't say anything into the cordless phone until I got to the den and sat on the couch.

"You know Mark is gonna be pissed as hell at you for breaking his sleep."

"I know. He's a light sleeper. Anyway, I wasn't going to ask you to do this, but I need you to watch Brandi for me tomorrow."

I knew I hadn't heard her right. I sat on the leather sectional with my feet tucked underneath my legs. The room was cold. Marcus and I never left the heat on when we slept. It was wasted energy; that's what blankets were for. "You didn't call me in the middle of the night to ask me that. You could have called me in the morning." I thought about it. "No, better yet, you should have called me earlier in the week."

"No," Shaundra said defiantly. "You need to take it up with Brenda."

"It's too late for this, Shaun."

Shaun's voice got noticeably louder. "Paul and I planned this trip a month and a half ago. Brenda agreed to watch Brandi because Niecee kept bullshitting and telling me that she wasn't sure if she was going to have plans that weekend. Then Brenda left me a message tonight saying that she wasn't going to be able to do it. And that's all she said."

I yawned. Unfortunately, I was starting to wake up. Ever since I'd seen Darius it had been taking me till forever to fall sleep. "That doesn't sound like Brenda," I said.

"Brenda has been trippin' lately, Shay, if you haven't noticed. I don't know what is wrong with the girl, but now I don't have anyone to watch Brandi, and I can't leave her here alone with Niecee."

I knew I was hearing things. "Niecee? Shaundra, you told me you were kicking Niecee out."

Immediately I heard Shaundra's attitude. "Just drop it, Shay. Will you watch Brandi or not? If you can't, I just won't go."

Shaundra was a smooth one. She liked to build her guilt trips slowly, then snafu your ass at the last moment.

"When you first called, you said that you needed me to watch her tomorrow. Did you mean that, or did you really mean the whole weekend?"

"Thank you, Shay. I appreciate this so much. Not the whole weekend, just Friday and Saturday night. We'll be back Sunday afternoon."

"Whatever, Shaun. What time do I need to be there?"

"Six. Brandi will fix her own dinner, so don't worry about that. I just want to make sure she doesn't have that little Negro up in my house, and she can't have company or go out with anyone, anywhere."

"Okay, Shaun. I'm going back to sleep. I'll be there tomorrow."

I found the remote control buried in the side of the couch and turned the television on.

When I arrived at the house on Friday night, Brandi couldn't have been happier to see me. She unlocked the front door, rolled her eyes, then went straight to her room and slammed the door shut. Wonderful godmother that I am, I was more than content. *Good riddance*, I said in my head, and rolled my suitcase into Shaundra's bedroom. Brandi didn't need to like me—though it did hurt my feelings that her attitude had changed so much toward me in the last few months. Now I was just an ally of her mother; screw all the godmommy stuff. I checked around the house. Niecee's room door was open, but she wasn't in the room and her raggedy-ass car wasn't outside, so that meant she wasn't home. I was relieved. Besides Niecee's twisted since of humor, everything else about her got on my nerves, so I hoped that she would be gone for the weekend.

I opened up the refrigerator and found a crystal dish with just enough banana pudding in it to give me a nice sugar high. I took the entire bowl to the couch with a large spoon and commenced to get my grub on. After about two hours, I heard Brandi stirring. By then I was watching a bootleg copy of *Footloose* that Shaundra had recorded on a VHS tape along with *Endless Love*. I tipped the sound down a little. First Brandi went to the bathroom, then to the kitchen. I heard the word *damn* as soon as she opened the refrigerator. She must have been looking for the last of the banana pudding. I laughed, but only loud enough for myself to hear. I had licked the bowl clean; there wasn't a drop left. *Pobrecita*. After a few seconds she stomped her little self down the hall again, and this time, after she slammed the room door, I didn't hear from her for the rest of the night.

Niecee didn't get home until the next morning after eight o'clock. I knew it was after eight because Shaundra's alarm clock set up in the bathroom said 7:23 the last time I had gotten up and I had been asleep again for the better part of an hour. I peeked out the door just to make sure Brandi wasn't trying to make a great escape. Mine and Niecee's eyes made contact.

"Good morning," I said, no particular expression on my face.

Niecee smirked and closed her door. I left Shaundra's door slightly open.

No wonder Shaundra needed a vacation. I couldn't even comprehend how she lived in a house with two attitudinal folks who didn't pay rent. I got back into bed. That was Shaundra's problem. I had enough of my own shit to deal with.

The day passed pretty evenly. I made breakfast around eleven for myself and left enough for Brandi if she got hungry. Niecee ate it. Brandi temperamentally opened and closed her door all day long; Niecee did the same thing, but in a more I-don't-give-a-fuck kinda way with less attitude. Since I was there to observe everything and make sure that things stayed cool, I left Shaundra's door cracked. Shaundra's computer was in the living room, and I used that as an excuse not to work on my novel. I told myself that I just didn't want to take a chance on running into either one of them. That was true, but it wasn't the crux of why I wasn't handling my business. Had I really wanted to write, I could have scratched down ideas on a notepad. Really, I was still tripping over everything going on with Darius and Marcus. Even though it was just mental, I didn't know how I'd managed to get my husband caught up in a triangle. I didn't know how I'd managed to get caught up myself. Though I still had deep feelings for Darius and I definitely had a sexual attraction, Darius was a jailbird at best. I sat on the edge of the bed with an empty notepad in my hand. Since I wasn't going to write, I started scribbling things:

Shay loves Darius.
Shay used to love Darius.
Darius is a punk-ass bitch who left me hanging.
Mark is good to me.
Shay should love Mark more.
Shay loves Mark.
Shay should stay with Mark.
Shay should go to church with Mark
Shay should go to church.

I wasn't going to solve anything tonight. As I kept writing, I started coming up with things I really didn't want to hear from myself. I put the notebook down and stared at the pole in front of me. I smiled. It was the first time I had smiled all day. I left the catch unlocked, but closed Shaundra's door a little bit more so that if anyone passed through the hall, they wouldn't see me doing my thing.

I turned on the clock radio in Shaundra's bathroom instead of the stereo on her dresser. I figured if the music came from the other room, I could hear Niecee and Brandi better if things got out of control. A song was on that had a lot of bass: "Freak-a-leek." I was about to break it down.

I figured, if I was really going to choreograph a pole routine for Marcus, I need to get to poppin'. I already had on sweats and a T-shirt, so I was comfortable enough. I took off my socks and placed them on the bed. "Freak-a-leek" spurred me on in the background. After I had practiced my walk a few times, I slid my hands up and down the pole practicing my smokeys. The music was jammin'. I began doing my old staple dance: the freak. My braids moved in little spirals. I hit my plunges with a quickness, then lowered my moves to the ground. From an almost split, I realized that I wasn't half as flexible as I used to be.

"Not bad," Niecee said, standing in the doorway with her arms crossed over a braless wife-beater tank.

"What do you want?" I said, not wasting any time.

Niecee smiled. "Nothin'. Just checking out what me and Brandi's babysitter is up to."

I sat up, but left my legs in a weak V. "You wouldn't need a babysitter if you would respect the house rules. Didn't you learn that shit as a kid?"

"No," Niecee said, unmoved.

"Well, you should have."

"You know," she said, "if you stretched out your groin muscles and hamstrings, you would be able to get a much better split." Niecee walked into the bedroom and sat about four feet from me on the carpet. "Look." Niecee tucked her left leg into her crotch area, then straightened her right leg in front of her and bent over. She held her stretch a few seconds then arched her foot.

"I know that stretch from junior high school, Niecee."

"Well, clearly you haven't been using it. It's really good for the hams." She flexed her feet then went into another stretch. "This one," she said as she lay on her back, "this one helps increase the limberness of the groin muscles and inner thighs, because gravity is working in opposition with you." Niecee opened her legs wide. The stretch looked like a split in the air. "You just let 'em hang." She glanced at me. "Try it."

I looked at her for a long second, then smirked. I pulled my shirt down over my sweats and reclined on my back. When I stuck my legs out into the air, I felt the stiffness.

"What's great about this is that you don't have to do anything, you just lay here, and if you do it every day for about thirty minutes, you'll be able to do a real split in about two to three weeks." Niecee placed both of her hands on her ankles and gently pushed both her legs to the ground.

I had been doing this for less than two minutes and it was hurting badly. "I can't do this for thirty minutes, Niecee. This mess hurts. My legs feel like they're going numb."

"Just massage them. Like this." Niecee pummeled her knuckles into her left inner thigh.

I pummeled my own thighs, but the pain wasn't subsiding. "I don't know if I need to do the splits that badly." I pulled my left leg over my right, then sat back up.

Niecee rolled her eyes. "Maybe this one will work better for you." She kept her legs in a split and rolled up so that she sat upright. "Put your feet against mine and give me your hands."

I gave her a look.

"Just try it and quit acting like some pain is going to kill you."

She lessened her split and I put my feet to hers and grabbed her hands.

"Now lean forward," she said.

"I'm going to fall."

"Shay, lean forward please and quit trippin'."

I leaned forward. I felt tension spidering through my inner thighs. Niecee leaned back, pulling my arms with her. My upper body hovered over the ground.

"This shit hurts. Damn."

"Ooohhhh, did Minister Mark's wife just let profanity slip from her precious lips?"

"Shut the fuck up, Niecee."

She laughed. I couldn't help giggling a little myself. Sometimes it was the most amazing thing in the world to me that I was married to a minister. I guess Niecee found it equally ironic.

She pulled my arms a little tighter. "Stripping, for real or for pleasure, as far as I am concerned, is all about stretching and keeping the muscles relaxed. If you keep your muscles in good condition, you know what they can do, so when it comes time to handle your business, you're not ever stressed. Your body is butter. My turn. Lock your palms."

I locked my palms. From the tension, she pushed me back up to a sitting position.

"Now you're gonna have to hold me at the elbows because I am a lot more flexible than you are."

I grabbed her elbows. Our feet still connected, Niecee started to execute her stretch. Because she was so limber, pulling her forward, I ended up lying all the way on my back. I was amazed at the shape she was in. I realized that though I wasn't fat or anything, and of our crew I probably had the next best body after Niecee, I was really slacking in comparison. Brenda was even starting to edge me out.

"Also, you can do the same basic thing we are doing now, against a wall or against the base of a couch, and you can also do it lying on your back."

"Thanks." I'd never really known Niecee to be so generous, but I had to be honest about the fact that I always tried never to be alone with her. Scorpios can be tricky; I knew that from dealing with Darius.

Niecee tried to increase her stretch. Her face inched dangerously close to my crotch. I didn't expect to—the stretch was completely innocent—but I was uncomfortable with her face being so close. I had bathed the night before, but I found myself wondering if I was fresh.

"That felt good," Niecee said, and she pushed herself back up.

Praise God, I thought to myself, and made my way back up.

"I can show you some basic pole stuff if you like." She stood up and adjusted her boxer shorts that said PRINCESS across the butt. "I'm in for the rest of the night, so it doesn't matter."

There are warning signs for everything. I should have gotten the hell out of Dodge while I had the perfect opportunity, but I didn't.

"If you don't mind," I said, "I'm trying to make up a little somethin'—somethin' for Mark to surprise him—and I only got a few moves from the class Shaundra and I took."

Niecee laughed.

"What's so funny?" I asked, feeling my sensitivity rise up.

"My bad. I'm just imagining Mark watching you pop your coochie before he heads off to Bible study."

"I don't have to defend my husband to you, Niecee. Mark is a preacher, but he's also a man."

"Like I said, *my bad*. Okay, the first thing I'm going to show you is how to swing properly from the pole."

I rolled my eyes. I was ready.

"This move"—Niecee glanced back at me—"is designed to give you a little hang time in the air."

I nodded.

She placed her right hand high up on the pole. "You're gonna grab the top of the pole with your right hand and go around a few times to pick up momentum. Then you put your right leg on the pole as high as you can, and lock the pole behind your knee.

You're gonna put your left hand under the leg on the pole, then swing."

Niecee spun in the air around the pole. As she came down toward the ground, she straightened out her top leg.

"You can come down with one leg straight or you can straighten them both so that the pole is sandwiched between your thighs. It's a nice visual."

What she had done was way more athletic and intricate than anything I had expected. It looked professional. I was impressed.

"Try it," she said, getting up from the ground.

I tried to get the order straight. I held on to the pole, locked my knee, and took off. I would say that Niecee tried not to laugh, but that would be giving her too much credit.

"Damn," I said, plopping to the carpet.

"You wanna get a good rotation going before you jump on the pole. That will increase your spin, and a good grip will increase your hang time. Also, it's easier to do if you have shorts on because your skin creates more friction against the pole than sweats do."

I wasn't about to take my sweats off. I tried it again.

"Much better," she said.

"Shut up, Niecee."

"Really. You had a little hang time and that basically looked right."

I gave her a look to see if she was telling the truth.

"*Really*," she said again. "Do it one more time."

The third time actually felt good to me. It felt like I was close to getting it right.

"Now." She came over to adjust my body on the floor. "When you land you wanna do something sexy like a spread eagle. When you bring your legs off of the pole, sit up on your elbows, open your legs wide, and point your toes. It gives the illusion of really long legs. See, this is where those exercises I gave you come in handy. You should be able to do this without even thinking about it."

I pulled my legs from around the pole and attempted a split on my back. My inner thighs were still sore and stiff. Niecee bent down in front of me.

"There," she said, arching my foot with her hand. "You break the line when your feet are flexed, and it looks unpolished. Keep them pointed. Practice, you'll get it."

After that, we worked on the *pushup, showgirl,* and a *baby booty clap.* I had worked up a serious sweat under my arms and across my back. It felt good. *Maybe this is what I needed,* I thought, *some exercise to clear my mind.*

"You ready for some lap dance tips to make Minister Mark hot?"

The way Niecee said things always made them sound dirty. I especially hated to hear Mark's name come out of her mouth. There was always something unsaid behind it. Inside of myself, whatever that unspoken thing was, I knew it had more to do with me than it did with Mark. It was like Niecee knew something I didn't.

"Are you down for lessons or what?" Niecee sat on the edge of Shaundra's bed staring at me. I hadn't ever taken her to be a person who cared about much, but it seemed like she cared about whether or not I let her help me.

"I think I need to take a nap." I forced a fake yawn.

Niecee rolled her eyes. "Anyway, the whole point of the lap dance is to turn the man on. You're his fantasy in the flesh and he needs to see that you like the advances he is making toward you. Sit down."

Damn. I limply walked over to the bed and sat down. Niecee doubled back to the bathroom to turn the radio up.

"Yeah, that's the shit," she said standing directly in front of me. She bent her knees and closed her eyes. The movement seemed to start in her waist. She rolled her wife-beater-clad stomach side to side, then in an elliptical fashion that made it look like she was moving her waist up and down and round and round at the same time. I'd always known that Niecee was a good dancer, but what struck me most now was her confidence. She was completely in her own groove and it didn't matter that I was watching. She opened her eyes and stepped closer to me. She stood in the space between my legs.

"What you want to do first is make sure that he knows that *you know* that you're sexy." She rubbed both of her hands over her breasts then licked her lips at me. She stepped closer again. "Remember the *pushup* move I showed you for working the floor?"

I nodded.

"Well, you can do that same basic move on a man's lap." She placed each hand on one of my thighs and scooped her head down and between my legs and slowly came up again.

I was paralyzed.

"When you are coming up, if the man has on a shirt with buttons, it is always nice to place one of his buttons in your mouth and look up at him." Niecee glanced up at me, then turned around. "It makes him think you want him," she said into the air in front of her. She shook her booty in my face. "The second you sit on his lap, you have to really work it, be in tune with the music, but make it a sensual grind."

Niecee sat down on my lap and began to move her butt around in my crotch area. If I was uncomfortable before, I definitely was more so now.

"I think I got the picture," I said, my body stiffening.

"All right," she said, wiggling her body up from my lap. "Your turn."

I laughed. "I've had all the turns I am going to get, Niecee. I'm about to go to sleep."

"Not without showing me what I taught you. Besides, this is for Pastor Mark, right? You wanna drop it like it's hot, don't you?

I did want to drop it like it was hot; that was the problem. I needed to. Mark and I needed it. I needed to find my husband sexy again. I needed him to find me sexy. Darius, who had absolutely no right to, was creeping back into my panties and my heart.

I envisioned myself giving Niecee a lap dance. I laughed again, but out of nervousness this time. "This is too embarrassing, Niecee. You are a girl. I can't do that to a girl."

"I'm your customer, your patron; it doesn't matter what sex I am. The whole point is that you need to satisfy the need. That's what a stripper does."

Clearly my true stripper mentality wasn't kicking in yet. I shook my hands out, then dried the developing moisture on my sweatpants. "So just start moving, huh?"

"Make your customer know that you know you're sexy."

I couldn't get over my embarrassment, so I tried to pretend like it wasn't there. I slowly moved into a freak-dance–inspired body roll. I let my hips make loose gyrations into the air. I placed my hands on my hips, then on my thighs, then back to my hips. I kept moving, but it seemed like my hands were completely out of place. I didn't know what to do with them, but I didn't want them anywhere near my breasts or private patch. I opened my eyes and glanced at Niecee, who was sitting on the bed again. She looked tense and expectant. My dance had to be the most boring thing in the world. The feeling of comfort just wasn't coming. I threw my hands down from my hips and forced my body to an abrupt stop.

"Okay, Niecee, I'm done. This is too awkward."

"No, you're not done," she said matter-of-factly. She pulled my hand and guided me to her. "Lap dance."

I stood sideways between her legs, for a moment not moving. She slapped my ass. "Get it going," she said.

In the back of my mind, I think I had always thought of stripping as something that was automatic and that didn't require any real energy or preparation. I bit into my lip and turned around so that my behind was facing her.

First, I moved my body in loose waves, like I was trying to

charm her with my apple bottom. Then I rolled my neck. I slid my hands up my thighs, up my stomach, past my ribs, and finally, my hands touched my breasts. It felt strange doing it in front of her. I closed my eyes and thought about what I had learned in Imani's class.

"Good," Niecee said. "Get free."

The confirmation was oddly encouraging. I kept my hands on my breasts and began to deepen my body roll. I turned my feet sideways and bent my back, so that she could see the arch.

"Good," she said again. "Work it, Shay."

Something in the music started to make sense to me. Though I was moving slowly and methodically, I was in my groove. I felt like I was a snake charming myself. Niecee became backdrop for me. I tried the *booty clap*, though I had just learned it minutes before. My butt didn't do a standing ovation, but it did give me a small clap of praise. I had to smile. Mark wasn't going to know what hit him.

A split second later, I didn't know what hit me. Niecee pulled me gently by the waist and led me to her lap. I continued my roll. The proximity had changed things. Now that I was dancing on her lap, I could smell the perfume on her neck mixing with baby powder and maybe the faintest hint of Alizé. She brushed her hands up my waist and gave me a chill. I kept dancing. There was no talking now. But I could hear her breathing and I could hear my own. She pulled me into her body more and at one precise moment, she placed her hand on my face and turned it toward hers. Our lips touched. I still didn't move. Her tongue went into my mouth and I let it. I accepted the energy. It was her right hand on my left breast that snapped me out of it.

"No, Niecee." I jumped up and put my hand to my lips. I turned back toward her. There she sat on Shaundra's bed in her gray wife-beater and princess boxers looking at me like absolutely nothing was wrong and absolutely nothing had happened.

"Why did you do that?" I asked her.

"Why did you let me?" she replied back.

I stood there speechless. I wasn't a dumb girl and I had never claimed to be, but had I just let Niecee kiss me? I had to think about it, assess it, mull it over. Get away from her. This shit was too much.

"I didn't let you kiss me, Niecee, and you know it."

Niecee got up from the bed. The expression on her face conveyed that she was entirely tired of playing with me. "You liked it. That's why you let me do it. Deal with that." In classic Niecee fashion, she licked her lips and walked toward the door. "Oh, yeah, Pastor Mark should absolutely love your dancing. Let me know if you want more lessons."

I climbed into the middle of Shaundra's bed. Though I was completely clothed, I felt naked. Sweat coated my body under my clothes. Confusion planted itself in the center of my head in the form of a migraine. As much as I tried to think and process what was going on in my life, the music from the radio was the only thing that caught my attention. "Drop It Like It's Hot" was playing in the background. I was going down with a quickness.

33

Brenda was excited. It had been too long since she had had a man next to her in her bed. She wondered if they would go to her place or to his. She wondered if he would stay the entire night and wake up with her in the morning or leave immediately afterward. She hoped he would stay. She could make them both coffee—hers imitation, his real. She didn't have any real coffee at home, though. She'd probably have to stop off at the store on the way home or tip out early in the morning before he woke up. And then again, if they went to his place, she wouldn't have to worry about any of that.

"You're getting ahead of yourself, Brenda," she said, zipping up the royal blue jogging suit jacket in the mirror. She looked pretty to herself, even with the feathered eye mask on. It had been so long since she'd actually felt pretty, the idea of it made her linger longer at the makeup station. Strange as it seemed to her, she wondered if he would expect her to take her mask off. She always left the club with a mask. She didn't take it off until she had cleared the club by a few good miles on the highway. It made sense to her that a man she liked and was about to have sex with would want see her face; she might even *want* him to see it, but that was a bridge she didn't need to cross yet.

This was it. She was going to have sex with someone she barely knew, but wanted to know more. She walked back to the bench in front of her locker and started to place her things inside her bag. The idea of having sex with him first was backward, she knew, but wasn't that how everyone did it nowadays? Why be different? She was tired of having her values date back to 1942. She needed to bring herself forward. She was determined to.

When Brenda walked down the long hall, back into the club, Bruce was waiting for her at the bar.

"You ready?" he said, catching the bartender's ear.

"Yeah," Brenda said back, looking past Bruce, at the bartender. Edward gave her a look. She nodded yes, that she was okay. He shook his head. Brenda flipped him a smile. She wasn't close to Edward, but they'd developed a respect for each other over the past few weeks. She knew that he liked her and had her back.

One of the bouncers always walked Brenda to her car at night; protection was the reason the strippers tipped bouncers in the first place.

"You cool?" Jason said to her as she exited the front entrance.

"I'm fine, Jason; thanks for asking."

"Would you like me to carry your bag?" Bruce asked as they walked around the side of the building.

"That's okay," Brenda said, then bit her lip. "I'm used to carrying it anyway."

"Well, my mother wouldn't have raised me right if I didn't ask."

Brenda nodded. She could smell the whiskey on his breath even when he wasn't facing her when he talked. She'd gotten used to the smell of alcohol. Pretty much every man she danced with during the evening had some flavor on his breath. But Bruce was special. She'd never kissed a customer before, and she had never thought of going all the way with any of them except for him.

Brenda stopped at the row where her car was parked. "Whose house do you want to go back to?" she said nervously. She found it hard to look Bruce in the face now. Instead she looked at his chest; the first four buttons of his silk shirt were undone.

He shrugged his shoulder as she opened her trunk. "Let's give it a little thought. Wanna sit in my SUV for a minute and decide?"

Brenda nodded again and placed her stripping bag in the back of her perfectly organized trunk.

Bruce's car was toward the front of the building and Brenda's was parked in the back of the lot. As they walked toward Bruce's

SUV, neither one of them touched. It bothered Brenda slightly; she would have loved to have held hands with him or had him drape his arm around her shoulder like she was his possession. Instead, they walked side by side with enough room for a thin child to squeeze between them.

"Here we are," he said, squeezing the disarm button on his remote. His car looked so new in comparison to hers. She felt ashamed that she had held on to her bucket of a car for so long, despite the fact that it still ran perfectly.

Bruce opened the driver's side backseat door and Brenda jumped in. Bruce climbed in behind her. Brenda adjusted her mask, then sat with her hands on the seat. The tan leather was nice; it complemented the blazing black exterior.

"I have a couple movies we could watch." Bruce looked up at the monitor suspended between the two front seats. "*Blade II* and *Mad Max Beyond Thunderdome*. You down?"

She wasn't into action flicks. Either one sounded boring enough to make her long for a good romantic comedy. "*Blade* sounds like it could be nice."

"Man, that's my shit," he said popping it from the DVD case into the player.

The previews started to roll and Brenda was beginning to wonder about his intentions. The man had just started a movie in a strip club parking lot. She took a deep breath. "You know, two hours is a long time to sit in a parking lot with no heat on. It's probably going to get a little cold."

"Your diction is so crisp," he said. "I like that about you. You sound educated, not like a ghetto girl." He scooted closer. "I got you, Mardi; I'm gonna keep you warm."

At that precise moment, it occurred to her to get out. He didn't even know her real name. She didn't know if Bruce was really his.

He slipped his arm around her back and it came up under the jacket of her sweatsuit. He brought his mouth to hers and kissed her.

Brenda kissed him back, but not with the passion she had kissed him with in the club.

Bruce squeezed more firmly around her waist. His strength felt good to Brenda. She softened into him a little more; he in turn gave more tongue. She began kissing him back for real.

"Yeah, girl. You do it for me, Mardi."

She wanted to *do it* for him; he did it for her. Everything about him seemed to be what she wanted. He was handsome, sweet enough, aggressive enough, employed, listened to his momma. What more could she really ask for?

As their session got more heated, Brenda thought about it. She could ask him if he had a girlfriend. She'd never thought about it for real until now. Bruce placed his hand under the soft rim of her bra onto her bare breasts. She quaked.

He couldn't have a girlfriend, she thought. Wouldn't he be spending his nights off with her? She pursed her eyelids and kissed him harder to shake the unknowns from her head.

"Yeah, baby," Bruce said, angling his body more toward hers. "Enjoy this shit. Let me please you."

Being pleased felt so good, Brenda thought.

Bruce braced her neck, then let his fingers inch up into her hair. Her entire body tightened up. She didn't want him to feel her tracks. She began to pull away.

Bruce held her immovably close. "It's okay, my last girl had a weave. Y'all gotta do what you gotta do." He anchored his fingers into her hair, then his left hand struck under the ribbing of her sweats, straight for her spot. It took him a couple of seconds.

"Girl, your pussy feels good and tight. It's already ready for me." Bruce jabbed in his index and middle fingers a few times, then added a third. Brenda tilted her head back against his hold. The leather seat squeaked under her. It felt good, yet at the same time, it felt like he was about to split her open. She hoped he wasn't about to try his entire fist.

Bruce let go of her hair and pulled his fingers out of her

vagina. He grabbed on to the ribbing of her pants and began to pull them down.

"I need to take off my tennis shoes," Brenda interjected. She didn't want her first time with him to be in his SUV.

"Cool, go ahead," he said. She started to pull off her shoes, but part of her expected that he would help her. He sat there, on his knees, expectant. Brenda got off her shoes and placed them on the mat below her seat. Bruce began to take off her pants again.

"Do you want me to take off my mask?" Brenda asked.

"I like the intrigue, makes me feel like I am having sex with a stranger, a woman I've never seen before."

Brenda's legs stiffened. "You never *have* seen me before; you don't even know my name." She crossed her hands over her chest.

"Baby," he said softly, and kissed her on the cheek. "I'm not in a rush. Everything in time. I will know your name, your address, what you look like without a mask, and what it feels like to wake up in your bed. Let's just relax. All right?"

Now they were getting somewhere. Brenda relaxed her legs and let him get the sweats and underwear over her ankles. He unzipped his pants, but didn't take them all the way off. He pulled a strip of condoms from the seat pouch facing the backseat. He tore one off. It was on.

The tip went part of the way in, then the whole penis. Brenda squirmed. He immediately started to speed up. As he pummeled into her, his breathing got heavier and heavier. It felt good to have his penis inside her—she guessed. She was so distracted, the penetration felt almost superficial. He was inside of her; she felt the stretching in her vagina, but the joy and pleasure wasn't tangible.

"Give me all of this hot, free pussy, baby. Make me come in your cunt, girl."

Brenda built up her nerve. "You wouldn't be here with me if you had a girlfriend, would you?" she said, staccato.

Bruce kept gyrating. "Shhh. Don't mess up the flow. Fuck me back."

Brenda scooted up on her arms a little, freeing her face from his shoulder. "I'm serious. You don't, do you?"

"No," he said, pressing her face back into his shoulder. "You okay now? You gonna let me fuck this pussy right? You gonna give it to me like only you can, baby?"

She nodded into him and instead of listening to his breathing, she concentrated on his answers. *He doesn't have a girlfriend* — she kept repeating in her head. Blade's voice played low in the background.

34

There are a few times in your life where every move that is made has the ability to change your life drastically. When Darius went to jail the first time was one of those times. When I married Marcus was one of those times. This moment was one; I could feel it every time I breathed. My life was on the cusp of disaster and I needed to bring it back. Only problem was, I didn't know where to bring it back to. I hadn't been happy in so long. To run back through my past and find the last moment I felt real and alive in wasn't realistic. High school was another lifetime ago. And the fact that I hadn't been able to secure happiness since then was a sad commentary on my life.

It had been a few days since the thing with Niecee. I had told Shaundra that I would wait till she got home that afternoon, but I hightailed it out of there before six o'clock in the morning. I wouldn't even allow myself to think about it. I didn't like women *like that*; I didn't even like Niecee at all, but the fact that I allowed her to kiss me was too much for me to handle. Not that I could have ever talked to Mark about this, but if I could have, if I would have just been a member of his congregation and not his wife, he would have told me to pray, that this situation was between me and God. I've heard him do it before during phone consultations with members of his congregation. I wondered what his face would have looked like when I told him that God and I stopped talking a long time ago.

The phone ringing knocked me out of my daze. I'd slept away most of the last few days and I didn't have much energy to do anything. The pole, which had usually perked me up, sat in its case untouched. Now, it reminded me of Niecee. From my side of the bed, I checked the caller ID and picked up. It was Brenda. I didn't feel like talking, but I managed to catch the call on its last ring.

"Hey, girl," I said into the phone.

"Shay, is this a good time?"

I thought about having an attitude. Had Brenda just kept her word to Shaundra about watching Brandi, the stuff between me and Niecee never would have happened. I wouldn't even have been there. "Yeah, what's up?" I asked, tightening my voice a little.

"Nothing, just calling to see what you are doing. We haven't talked in a few weeks."

Brenda never called about *nothing*. I wondered if she knew that about herself. "I'm glad you called, girl; I've left you a couple of messages, but don't seem like a sistah can get a return phone call." I placed Marcus's pillow under my head and turned onto my back.

"I know, Shay. Things have been a little hectic lately. I've been . . ."

I waited for her response.

"I've just been swamped lately."

"Ummm," I said, leaving Brenda to stew in her own juices. If I let her play possum enough, she would show herself.

"Shay, court's about to start up again in ten minutes. I just wanted to—"

"What, Brenda?" I said, showing my first inkling of curiosity.

Brenda paused. I could hear her breathing pattern clearly in the receiver; it was rushed. "I met a man, Shay."

I wanted to tell her to run like hell, but maybe that was the advice I should have given myself. "That's good, Brenda; is he nice?"

Brenda's voice got low. "We had sex the other night."

We both got quiet.

You did what? was my internal response, but again, I caught myself. I had to sit up for this. "How long have you known him, Bren?"

"A few weeks, but it's okay. I feel good about it. The sex was great."

I felt like a parent. Had this been Shaundra or even Karina, I would have been happy for them, but Brenda—Brenda was different. Heart on her sleeve wasn't the half of it. When it came to liking a man, she was an easy mark.

"I don't know what to say, Bren, other than to be careful and use protection."

She sensed my apprehension. "You didn't even ask his name, Shay. If I was Shaundra, you would have asked a thousand questions. Okay, I just wanted to check in, no biggie. I'll call you later—"

Before I could get another word in, she had hung up. I leaned back into the pillows again. How was I going to help guide anyone else's life when I couldn't fix my own? I rolled over to grab the remote from the nightstand. It was time for *The Young and the Restless.*

35

Shaundra sat on the floor Indian-style looking through Brandi's letters. She had already gone through all of her coat pockets and checked under the mattress. She wasn't being nosy, at least not outright. She was protecting her family. Her child. Ever since the big fight over Brandi having a boy in her room, things had been different between them. Worse than different. Shaun had never imagined herself feeling like an outsider in her own home, around her own kid. She would tiptoe around to hear corners of conversations between Niecee and Brandi. She would cook Brandi's favorite foods and order in pizza only to have it grow dry, stale, and uneaten in its carton.

It seemed like the more she tried to make amends, the more Brandi resisted. Brandi barely even spoke to her anymore. And when she did speak, it seemed like there were always dollar signs attached. Snooping was her only option.

Shaundra found four origami-style letters and two single-sheet letters pressed into the pages of her notebook. She read through the first one. If she had had any doubt that her daughter was having sex, she could put it to rest. Seemed like Brandi did the do as regularly as Shaundra did herself. She and her girlfriend Latisha exchanged stories graphically. She raised herself from the floor and made her way to the kitchen. It was only twelve o'clock in the afternoon, but it was Shaundra's belief that there are some things that only a good drink can get you through. Tears weren't going to help. She didn't even know about prayer or straight whuppin' Brandi's ass.

Shaundra had met Latisha a few times, even dropped her off at her grandmother's house after basketball games, but she would have never known that Latisha was such a nasty-ass with such a fresh mouth. The girl yes-ma'amed and no-ma'amed Shaundra, even when she called on the phone. In writing she was scandalous, as scandalous as Shaundra's own daughter.

Shaundra wondered. Had she and Shay been that bad back in the day? She took the quarter bottle of Jack with her back into Brandi's room. She didn't want to think about it. Shaundra and Shay both had started having sex in high school, Shay at fifteen and Shaundra three months and two days after turning sixteen. Shaun folded one of the letters back into its shape and shook her head. Brandi had gotten a better upbringing than this. If nothing else, Shay, Shaundra, and Niecee could testify without a doubt that they had practically raised themselves. They were survivors. Shaundra had tried to make Brandi's life different. Even after she and James divorced, she had tried to give Brandi all of the stability she'd never had.

She opened up another letter and read it through. Shaundra felt like she had been coping well up until that point, but she wished she'd never found this one.

"Help me, Jesus," Shaun said into the air. She hugged the letter close to her heart.

36

I had decided; I was ready to have a baby. Okay, maybe I wasn't ready, but I was pushing ahead anyway. Marcus was ready; he had been ready for a long time. Secretly, I think that's what he thought I needed—someone to calm me down. Someone to depend on me. Maybe he was right, but I tried not to think about his reasons. I had my own.

With a baby, I wouldn't be able to move backward. I would have to move forward, and that would mean getting rid of Darius once and for all. I could do that. I needed to for my own sanity. A baby would break Darius and me apart once and for good. I would be what I was never really sure I wanted to be—a normal housewife.

I thought about this as I sat in bed rereading Darius's last letter. He missed me. He was so happy I had finally come. He wanted me to come back. He couldn't wait till we were *together-together* on the outside. I couldn't go through this anymore. The pulling I felt was tiring me out.

Niecee had called to make sure I knew his letter had come and that I could come get it without thinking she was going to do something to me. I knew I shouldn't have even needed to read it. But I did, though. I was going to explode or collapse or crack up or something if I didn't.

When I made it to Shaundra's house, in the middle of the day, exactly thirty-three minutes after Niecee's call, the awkwardness set back in. I didn't want to see her. I didn't want her to see me. I had on a pair of blue jeans with apricot paint dried onto the legs from painting the hallway a color Marcus hated. The back of my braids still looked good, but the front, if you looked closely, really did need to be redone. The strangest part of me wanted to look good for her, and the whole idea of that seemed absolutely insane. I flipped down the driver's side mirror and applied the slightest bit of Vaseline to my lips. When I got to the door, I was relieved. I saw an envelope jutting from the mailbox. I pulled it out. If a neighbor had been watching me, she probably would have sworn I was stealing mail, the way I snatched the letter and did a run-walk to the truck. I got inside and drove ten or twelve blocks away before I stopped at a random curb. I flipped the letter over to open it and noticed writing across the flap that wasn't Darius's. Purple ink said: *I told you I wasn't going to mess with your silly behind. Have a good one. Let me know the next time you want strip lessons. Hope your thing with Pastor Mark goes well.* I didn't trust her as far as I could throw her.

Back at home, on my side of the bed, where I had been spending a lot of time lately, I reflected on his letter again. His words made me sad. I suppose his letters had always brought on sadness, but this time, I couldn't feel the excitement that had always been beneath it.

It hurt me that I was about to give me and Darius up. What made it hardest was that I should have done it a long time ago. Even before I married Marcus. I wiped the tears from my cheeks with the back of my left hand and lay back down. I didn't want to masturbate to calm my nerves. I didn't want to watch television to distract myself. I wanted to be still. Really still. I was going to become a real and complete wife to Marcus once and for all.

37

Shay hadn't even asked Bruce's name. How many times had Brenda sat through Shay and Shaundra telling stories about their men? She'd been listening to them since junior high school. She'd laughed and cried with them. She'd held Shay's hand when Darius went to jail and Shaundra's when she and James divorced. Brenda thought about the inequity in her relationships the entire freeway ride to work. She was tired of being background. All she had wanted was for Shay to listen, the same way she had always listened to Shay—with respect.

Brenda clicked her right signal and merged onto the off-ramp. She wasn't going to let Shay's insensitivity get to her. It was a special night. Bruce had asked her to come in to work just to see him. Tuesdays and Wednesdays were always slow, and they would have a lot of uninterrupted time together. She was glad that he wanted to spend time with her, though it would have been nice to do something away from the club. A movie would have been nice, Brenda thought, maybe even dinner; she could have cooked.

Bruce was moving something on the inside of her that hadn't been stirred in a long time. She was starting to feel like a woman, not just some girl with a cardboard life. She had even had sex for the first time in more years than she cared to admit. Anything past two was too long a time not to have a man between her thighs. A long time not to feel kisses on the back of the neck. She had needs, even if she tried to pretend she didn't.

It didn't matter to her that their first time was in the back of his truck—in retrospect, it was special. Bruce's want for her had been tender but animalistic. He half took and he half asked. Before the actual penetration, he had even tried to motion her down on him. The logistics were a little hard to coordinate within the confined space, and her mask kept catching. Brenda laughed as she pulled into the lot. She circled a time and a half to see if Bruce's car was there yet. It wasn't. She could have gone down on him; a part of her even wanted to, the other part thought it was too risky. She didn't even know him. She didn't know anything about his sexual history, if he *really* had a girlfriend or a *wife*. He said he didn't, she reminded herself. Her mind kept flip-flopping. She wanted to fall, but another part of her wanted to play it safe. Getting involved with anyone from the club outside of work was risky. At the end of the day, no matter how she twisted it, no matter how far she got away from her center, she was still a peace officer. That didn't end just because she was at a club shaking her ass. In her mind she knew she was toeing a dangerous line. But her mind and her heart were different entities. Her heart wanted to be desired, and she felt that way every time she walked onstage. Her heart wanted this man, even at her own risk.

Brenda wanted Bruce to see her completely. Even though she felt comfortable being behind her mask, it was a barrier, and she wanted to reveal herself to him. She wondered if that was a mistake in judgment, if her entire relationship with him was a mistake. She thought back to a point during their lovemaking when he had knocked her mask down a little with his face. It was like he had been fucking a hooker and the condom had fallen off. He stopped mid-stride to place the feathers back in their proper position. All he said was, "Wouldn't want to lose the intrigue." What the hell was that supposed to mean? "Intrigue?" Her emotions were spinning from contentment to anger to confusion and back again. She sat in the driver's seat wondering what was happening to her. Her decisions had always been so safe and well thought out.

Though she didn't want to allow it, the biggest part of her felt used. What kind of man doesn't want to see the face of a woman he's dating? Brenda sucked in her breath. Okay, maybe they weren't dating, yet, but sex was a much bigger commitment than a movie. Sex was a much bigger commitment than a date. She continued to tap the steering wheel. There was a possibility that he wouldn't even show up tonight. She had never felt like the smartest pea in the pod, but she rarely felt stupid like she did now. She steadied herself. She'd tried to stop the negative self-talk in her brain. *Idiot. That's why he wanted to wait to exchange numbers; it wasn't that he didn't have a pen; it was that he didn't want you to call.* Her body trembled. *He doesn't want you on the inside of his world, that's all.* Brenda tried to stop the tears from flowing but it was hard.

Suck 'em up, she said to herself, imitating Shay. She wiped away her tears with the back of her hands. This wouldn't be the first almost-relationship to blow up in her face. Derek. Russell. The fat guy she didn't even like. She knew the drill. *Just let it go.* The pain would stop eventually. She tapped the steering wheel one last time, but she wanted to punch it. She needed to think about right now. Right now she needed to figure out whether she was going to go inside the club or go home. She did have court early in the morning. But if she went home, all she was going to do was watch TV and go to bed early. *I may as well stay*, she thought. She could go to bed early any night; besides, if she did go home, she knew that tears were unavoidable. At least this way, her mind would be distracted. At least this way she wouldn't feel weak. She would get the chance to wear her new purple feathered mask with hot pink beads framing the eyes. Brenda got out of the car. She promised herself another customer would never get that close to her again.

38

Shay wished that Brenda would just answer the phone and quit acting temperamental. Okay, she should have been more interested in her new guy. Granted. But Brenda had no idea what Shay had been going through the past few weeks herself. She wasn't trying to be selfish, but damn. Everything felt like life or death. Shay had never been through a time in her life that was so Jerry Springer–ready. From the way Brenda wasn't answering the phone, Shay knew she had an attitude. Brenda usually answered on the second ring, and Shay had been trying to reach her since Tuesday. It was now Thursday. Shay picked up the wireless phone sitting next to her computer monitor and dialed Brenda's number one more time. After four rings, the machine came on.

"This is my third message, Brenda. I apologized already. I *do* want to hear about this new man in your life. Just call me, all right? You know you can't keep a grudge. This is ridiculous."

When she pressed the END button, she had to let it go. Brenda could play possum, but Shay had business to take care of.

Shay smiled and caught the awkwardness of her expression in her reflection on the monitor. She looked afraid, and she felt more fear about this than she had about anything in a long time. She and Marcus were about to make a baby, and that one thing would change her life forever.

She got up from the desk and walked into the master bathroom. Shay sat on the toilet and stuck her middle finger inside of her vagina to remove her birth control ring. She looked at the opaque, rubber-band-sized ring in her hand. She stared real hard, then wrapped eight squares of toilet tissue around it and threw it in the trash. After three hours of not having the ring in her body, according to the pamphlet, she was supposed to use a backup form of birth control because she could be capable of getting pregnant. It was already five o'clock and Marcus would be home in less than an hour. She should have taken it out sooner, but now was the first moment that seemed right. Shay tried not to cry. This was supposed to be a happy occasion. An occasion where she would pull out all of the stops.

She'd assembled the pole in the bedroom earlier that morning. Now it was time for her to put on her costume. She knew a nurse's outfit wouldn't be the most original costume in the world, but it was one she would feel comfortable in. Besides, she would be dancing to Marvin Gaye, and who better to give sexual healing than a nurse. Shay stripped her five-foot-six-inch body bare and began to re-dress herself. The panties were white lace with cutouts in the crotch area; she slipped them on. She sat on the toilet and rolled the white fishnet stocking up each leg and attached the garter clips. Before the four-inch heels that seemed entirely too high, she put on the 36B white lace bra that matched the underwear and buttoned up the front of the mini nurse's uniform. Last things were her paper nurse's hat and the fake stethoscope around her neck. She looked at herself. She looked new. She felt the same way she felt when her uncle held her arm and walked her down the aisle. Shay breathed. She was about to rock Mark's world.

When Marcus walked through the front door, the curtains were drawn and the living room lights were dimmed.

"I'll get that," Shay said. She got up from her seat in the armchair and made her way to him slowly, partly so that his eyes would have time to adjust to her and partly so that she didn't fall trying to walk in those heels.

Shay kissed him on the cheek, then reached for his briefcase and dropped it to the floor.

"What is this?" Marcus said, a smile shining through his voice.

"It's baby-making attire," Shay said, and this time she landed her kiss on his lips. The pull away took a little bit too long. She kissed him again, then grazed his bottom lip with her teeth.

"We need to make babies more often then," Mark said, his lips still so close she could smell the deep-roasted scent of coffee on his breath. Marcus leaned his lips down to his wife's breasts. He kissed in between them, then got flashy and licked the spot above where the lace bra showed.

It took Shay a second to catch her breath. She closed her eyes and rode the tempo of her husband's lips. "I'm starting to think you're right; we should make babies more often. You know, I may not get pregnant immediately; we may need to keep trying." They both smiled.

She could feel a tingle deep inside her vagina. Shay had had this feeling before, but never with Marcus. It was something she wanted to hold on to. She kissed his lips one last time just to keep the feeling going. As gently as he could, Marcus snatched open the top button of the uniform and pressed his hand against the white lace. He scooped out the breast and began to suck.

Shay shuddered. The tingling spread into her chest. In the twelve years she'd known him, she'd never just wanted him with reckless abandon, but she wanted him that way right now. She wanted to fuck his brains out, suck him dry, then fuck him all over again, but the next time, with her on top. She took a deep breath. It took everything in her to push his head away from her breasts.

"Unh-uh," she said. "There's more in the bedroom." Shay took the same hand that had moments before been on her breast, into her hand. "I want you to close your eyes and not open them until I tell you, okay?"

"Whatever you say," he said.

She led him to the bed and sat him down on the bed before she turned the music on. Marvin Gaye's "Sexual Healing" and

Shay's sincere desire for her husband took over the air in the room.

"Now," she said.

When Marcus opened his eyes, he saw his wife, the first lady of his church, doing a bump 'n' grind against a stainless steel stripper's pole.

Shay licked out her tongue at him and then went in for the kill—the pole trick Niecee had taught her. She placed her right hand high on the pole, swung around a few times to gain momentum, locked her right leg onto the pole, and let the other leg swing. She felt like she was flying. As she slid down the pole, she kept both legs above her body so that the pole was sandwiched between her thighs. When she landed, Shay unwrapped her legs from the pole, and pressed them out spread eagle into the best split her stiff legs could muster. Her white lace cutout panties faced him.

Marcus stood up. "Just stop it, Shannah. That's enough."

Shay knew she couldn't be hearing right. She sat up; she wanted to look Marcus in the eye, but before she did, she stared down at his crotch. His penis was hard.

Marcus moved from in front of the bed over to the stereo system in the corner to turn off the music.

"What's wrong with you, Marcus?" Her face frowned up.

"What's wrong with *me*?" Marcus brought both hands to his chest. "My wife tells me she is ready to make a baby and I come into our sanctified bedroom and she's turned it into a den of hell and you ask what's wrong with me?"

Shay blinked her eyes a few times rapid fire. She'd worked so hard to make this right for Marcus and now he was standing in front of her, screaming.

"I thought—"

"You thought what? You thought I wanted this?" His voice was hard.

It took her a second to find her voice again. "I overstepped.

Forget it. I just wanted you to see a different side of me. That's all." She rolled up from the carpet and headed to the closet.

"I don't know what to say, Shay. I want this pole out of my house."

She grabbed a pair of sweats and headed into their joint bathroom. "Well, why don't you go pray about it; maybe it'll disappear." She slammed and locked the door. Her feelings were hurt.

Marcus raised his voice so that she could hear him through the closed door. His voice wasn't hard or cold; it was matter-of-fact. "That's exactly what I'm going to do. I suggest you do the same."

That wasn't what she was going to do. Shay didn't know what she was going to do yet, but whatever it was, she was going to leave God and Marcus out of it.

39

After she had thrown back three whiskey sours, she started to feel better. Actually, she almost felt good. Bruce could kiss her natural-born, caramel-colored, Olive Oyl–esque ass. She'd never drunk so many cocktails in such rapid succession. Instead of feeling queasy, her body felt relaxed and her mind had slowed to a pace where every single thing going on in her life seemed manageable. As far as her captain was concerned, she would make sure he never found out. As far as Shay was concerned, she wasn't going to listen to any more of her drama. And Bruce? Brucy-Bruce could go somewhere and fuck himself. The alcohol had made all things simple again. And before she did her last set onstage, she would be sure to throw back one more—for good measure.

The evening had passed smoothly as far as Brenda was concerned. She hadn't cried, and Bruce's carcass only entered her mind in small, erasable stints. Brenda felt as though she had truly elevated herself to true stripper status. She'd listened to the music each time she gave a lap dance, but she didn't allow the customers to touch her, not on the inside. They were as good as puppets with money in their hands. Her image of herself didn't rise and fall from their views of her. They were the anomalies, not her. They were the ones that needed saving. On evenings like this, when the club was a quiet ripple instead of a rush, Brenda had the freedom to determine what went on here at her own pace. This was definitely not a place to find love in. She didn't know what she had been thinking when she started to open up her heart to Bruce. At best, this was a place to alleviate and cultivate lust. At worst, this was somewhere that could break a girl or a customer down if they didn't pay attention. She knew that the girls were the ones who usually ended up wounded. She could tell that from her own behavior over the last few weeks. Sometimes, when she danced with the men, she tried to find a kindness in their eyes—something that communicated that they respected or at least understood something about her plight. Usually she just saw emptiness starring back at her, or something that was less than that, that almost scared her.

She was glad when she saw Luscious go up; she knew that she was up next, and at least tonight, she would get home before three. The mornings when she got off after sunrise always left her irritable, because she hated sleeping during the day. Something always seemed wrong with that, even on Saturday and Sunday. She had to work her *real job* in the morning, anyway. She wanted to be fresh; her judge was starting to notice her falling off her game a little.

When Luscious's second song began to play, Brenda excused herself from the floor and went to prepare behind the curtain. She thought about getting another drink, but changed her mind. She did a few side bends, rolled her neck, and warmed her knees so that her joints wouldn't pop audibly while she was on stage. Popping joints were never sexy. When her body was ready and Luscious was winding it down, Brenda went to take one last look at the crowd. As expected, customers had been light tonight, and the audience had gotten even thinner between midnight and one A.M. Depending on how many men sat around the stage, and what pattern they were in around the club, Brenda would adjust her stage show accordingly. Or she could do what it always seemed to her that Sparkle did, dance for herself and let the men catch a thrill whenever she aroused herself enough.

Brenda stood peeping out on the side of the curtain. Four men were around the stage, three at the bar, and six or seven were in various seats throughout. She would dance for the men around the stage and try to give little flourishes to the other men, enough to make them want to walk up to the stage and give tips. It seemed like the second before she released the curtain, she saw a six-foot-something dark-skinned brotha round the corner into the club. Brenda let go of the curtain quickly. She was sufficiently tipsy, but she could feel her mind speeding up and tightening again. She could shoot herself for not buying that fourth drink she had promised herself. If she had followed through with her plan, she'd have probably been high enough to barely even notice Bruce when he entered. She wrung her hands. *What am I going to do?* she thought. *Why do I need to do anything?* was her immediate response. It was Bruce who had flaked on her, not the other way around. She waited for Luscious's set to come to a close.

"Gentlemen, give it up for our own sexy, masked freak of the week, Mardi Gras."

Brenda danced onto the stage, but where she had been so sure moments ago, now she was shaky. She didn't want to, but almost organically, she glanced in Bruce's direction. He sat next to a white guy who looked vaguely familiar to her. Bruce's expression looked the same as it always had when he watched her dance—attentive and serious, like she was some type of goddess. She had to fight her inward desire to blush. *Stop it, Brenda,* she said in her head. She didn't want to be happy to see him; 1:30 in the morning was not what they had agreed upon for a meeting time.

She arched her back and rested her behind against the pole to do the *booty clap* with either butt cheek on either side of the pole. As much as she wanted it back, the relaxed, I-don't-give-a-fuck attitude that had come so easily with alcohol was quickly fading. She started rationalizing for him. *Technically we didn't set a particular time.* Maybe she had gotten the whole thing wrong. Maybe as far as he was concerned, he had kept his word. This wouldn't have been the first time she had overreacted. Brenda tried to concentrate on her dancing, but all she could really think about was him. And finally, when he smiled at her, she found herself smiling back.

Five minutes after she counted out the measly seventeen dollars she had made from dancing two songs, she kept the routine and went to the VIP room. Her gut was messing around with her heart. More than any other time in a long time, her gut told her to grab her shit and go home. Now. But she wanted to see Bruce. She wanted to see if his intentions had somehow increased since the last time they had seen each other. He had to have at least missed her. She had missed him so much; thoughts and images of him had clouded every moment of her life from the second they committed to have sex. Before Jimmy opened the door, he told her that she had two customers waiting, but when she walked in, she only saw one—Bruce. She wanted to yodel, she was so happy to see him.

"I thought you weren't going to show up," she said, adjusting her beautiful new mask on her face. She dropped her bikini top on the spare seat.

"Come on now," he smiled. "You do too much for me for that. Come here."

Brenda moved over to him. She straddled his lap and lowered herself onto him.

"That's what I'm talking about."

Brenda started her gyrations and Bruce's penis swelled between her legs.

"Did you miss me?" he asked.

"Yes." She nodded.

"Did I make you come good?"

She nodded yes again, but felt a little embarrassed this time.

"Did you miss me?" She pressed her body harder to his.

"How could I not miss this juicy pussy. Girl, are you crazy?" He kissed her, and with her whole self she kissed him back. Bruce pushed her up off him a little and glided her G-string to the side of her vagina.

Brenda thought to tell him no, but she wanted him.

She felt his knuckle and middle finger pass into her. He pumped.

"Ahmmm," she said, closing her eyes. This is why she had scheduled herself to come in on an off day. Her manless stint had gone on for too long.

"Your pussy is wet already," he said into her mouth as she kissed him.

"Yeah," she said, absorbing the moment.

"I want to fuck you." He moved his wet lips to her ear.

Brenda bit his neck. His skin was salty on her tongue. "Later. We can go to my house."

"Right here, Mardi. I want to do you right here."

"After." She kept kissing.

"You know how good it would feel. This spot's dead tonight; nobody is going to catch us. I want to fuck you, then stick my fingers up your ass and make you scream." Brenda didn't say anything. She was never much for booty feels. But maybe she would try—for him. Bruce took her silence as permission. He snapped his belt and unzipped. He pulled a strip of three condoms from his shirt pocket, tore one off, and placed the others on the cushion. The condom went on masterfully. He entered her. Brenda closed her eyes and rode the excitement of breaking the rules. Knowing clients were just outside the door somehow made it sweeter. His first song was just ending and already he was exactly where he wanted to be. But so was she. The only thing sweeter would have been for this to be happening in her own bed.

"Brenda, I want you to meet somebody." He said into her mouth, but somehow it didn't taste right.

"What?" she said, stopping her kiss.

Bruce lightly bit her lip. "A buddy of mine, Kenny. I told him about you."

With both hands Bruce held the sides of her face and began to kiss her again. And in the same instant, with Bruce's hands still on her face, she felt two hands on her shoulders. Then down her back. Then to the sides of her breasts. Brenda froze. She tried to move her hands, to push the other man's hands away, but she couldn't. Goose bumps rose on her skin.

"Don't be that way, baby. Loosen up." Bruce's hold on her face was growing tighter, and his penis still pounded into her. "Relax, you'll enjoy it. Double the wetness. Double the dick."

"Bruce, man, what's up? I paid a hundred dollars for this, man." Kenny seemed a little anxious.

"Mardi's my girl. She'll come around; won't you, Mardi? You'll at least suck his dick, right, baby?" He looked her in the eye and nodded yes, insisted yes.

Kenny's hands stuck to her breasts, and her hands were still glued around Bruce's neck. She couldn't move. Kenny lowered his lips to her neck. His sucking felt foreign. He bit her shoulder. "Turn her around, man." Kenny looked at Bruce.

Bruce pumped a few more times, hard.

He manipulated her. Turned her on his lap so that she now faced this man whom she had not invited to touch her body. She tried to think about everything her training had taught her. *Always check your surroundings. Trust your gut.* She should have listened. She stared at him one good time in the face before he lowered her face to his dick. Brenda felt Bruce's finger attempting to go up her ass. He twisted. Her gut knew what was coming. She'd had rape prevention training before. She was supposed to avoid situations that didn't feel right. She was supposed to say NO, in a way that made an aggressor know that she meant it. She was supposed to defend herself.

"No," finally came out. Kenny placed her mouth back onto his dick.

"This bitch better not bite me." He looked at Bruce again.

She was numb, but in all of her numbness, Kenny's familiarity was still there.

He held both sides of her cheeks and moved her face forward and backward. "I thought you said she would be game, man." He pumped his penis into her mouth.

"She is. I guess she ain't ever got down like this before. Every other stripper I've spent this kind of money on knows the deal.

What the fuck is a VIP room for, anyway?" He laughed through labored breath. With two fingers in her ass, he used his other hand to get his dick hard again. "Loosen up, Mardi, we'll be good to you. This is two hundred dollars, girl."

Brenda took a breath and closed her eyes.

They were starting to hit a good rhythm together: the white guy in front, Bruce pumping her ass from behind with his fingers. They had to have done this before. But she wasn't a whore, no matter how it looked. No matter what they were doing to her. She was a woman falling for a man she wanted to love.

"No, stop, please," Brenda said, and even though her speech pattern was obstructed, the guy in front knew what she was saying.

She didn't have to scratch him or bite him. She felt her words jolt his body, then he just backed off. His penis disengaged from her mouth.

"I'm not a rapist, man," he said, zipping up his pants and shaking his hands nervously like she'd spilled some hot grits on them. Bruce pushed her off him so that she landed on the cushion next to him like an empty suitcase. Brenda didn't move. Bruce didn't say anything, but under her own fear, she could smell theirs.

40

The night wasn't that cold, but Shay felt a chill all over her body. She reached one hand down from the steering wheel to turn the heater on. Strangely enough, with all the crying she had done over the last few weeks, she didn't feel like crying now at all. She was angry, but she wouldn't allow herself to feel that either. If she allowed herself to be angry, then she would have to admit that she was hurt. To admit she was hurt might lead to tears, and if she allowed herself to cry, she had no idea what might happen next.

At least this way, in this moment of disconnection, she could be impulsive. She didn't care about anything enough to stop and think. She wanted to roll. She wanted to walk on her freedom until she found the end of the line. Then she would turn back, if she wanted to. Whatever gods ruled this world of inbetweenness were working on her side, because when she got to her best friend's door, both Shaundra and Brandi were gone, and when Niecee answered, Shay asked if she could come in.

41

First thing she did when she got home was swab the inside of her mouth. She used three Q-tips, each end, then she placed them in a plastic bag. Next thing she did was swab her vagina. Then her ass. She walked to the spare bedroom, where most of her mother's old stuff was, and took pictures of her face with an old Polaroid. She remembered exactly which drawer the Polaroid camera was in.

She felt beat up, but more than anything, she felt like she had fallen. She had always lived a respectable life. A proper life. A life that some people might have wished they had had the opportunity to have. Good credit. Her home was paid off. Good friends. A stable career. Why did she have to go screw it all to hell? It didn't make sense. Nothing about this did. She grabbed a book and her police academy class graduation photo that was still lying facedown on the coffee table from when she set up the pole. Usually, she would have fallen asleep first on the couch and then transferred herself to her bed. Tonight, after the shower, after all the gentle brushes of the towel over her swollen lower region and throbbing face, she got into bed. It was almost daylight now. Had she looked through the drawn bedroom curtains, she would have seen the sky turning a loose gray.

After all the reasoning and rationales, she had no idea why she had done this to herself. She'd never understood why people jeopardized everything important to them for something that, in the end, wouldn't seem important at all. But stripping had been important to her. It was the only thing that had ever made her feel desired. Why did Bruce have to do this to her? Brenda involuntarily shook her head. Of all the things she had been in her life—awkward, rhythmless, plain—she had never been thought of as a whore to be passed around.

Brenda stared at the photograph. This had been her finest moment. The only day she imagined might be better would be her wedding day. She looked at herself all in uniform with the rimmed cap cutting just above her eyes. Her eyes were radiant. She had gone through more than 880 hours of training to become a police officer. She stared harder at herself in the photo, then scanned the faces of each of her forty-eight classmates. Only two other women had graduated in her class. The hell they went through to make it—the heckling, the names. Brenda placed the picture facedown on the floor and slid it under the bed. Any decisions she had to make would have to happen in a different lifetime, to a different woman. Now she needed some rest.

42

After leaving Niecee, Shay couldn't bring herself to go home. It was almost ten o'clock in the evening, and staying at Shaundra's or going home seemed like two of the worst options in the world. A hotel seemed like her best way out. Shay had money, but something in her didn't want to be alone. She would have called Brenda from her cell phone, but in the haste of leaving the house, she'd forgotten it on the kitchen counter. Maybe that was best, Shay thought. She didn't want the pressure of having to talk to Marcus tonight.

She sat in front of Brenda's house. Brenda's car was outside, but all of the lights, at least the ones visible from the front street, were off. Shay reclined back into the driver's seat. She wanted to knock, but she wasn't sure. And really, if she was honest with herself, the last thing she wanted to hear was joyful news about Brenda's new boyfriend. At this moment, love seemed like the worst curse in the world.

Shay got out of the car and made her way up the uneven walk, up four steps, to the door. She rang the doorbell once, then knocked two times. She waited. Nothing moved. She knocked again. It occurred to her that Brenda could still be mad at her.

"Brenda," Shay said, wedging her voice between the door and the frame. "Brenda, I know you're mad, but I need you. I just left Marcus." Shay leaned away from the door, and not until that moment did she start to cry. She hadn't consciously thought of her leaving that way, but when she said it to one of her dearest friends, from the heart, that is exactly what she meant. Shay stood there, leaning against the thin strip of wall between the door and the window. Just hours before she was about to make the leap

206 K i m o n a J a y e

into motherhood, and now, now her future looked completely blank. "Suck it up," she said aloud.

The front door opened behind her.

"I didn't think you were going to open up," Shay said, wiping her cheeks with her sweatshirt.

"I wasn't." Brenda unhooked the screen door.

Before the front door was closed good, Brenda and Shay embraced.

"I think I just left Marcus," Shay said into Brenda's ear. She hugged her tighter. "I'm sorry I've been so selfish. I should have listened to you when you called. It's just you were calling about this man, and that's the last thing I wanted to hear about at that moment. I'm sorry."

Brenda accepted her embrace. Shay could feel Brenda's tears on her neck. "He raped me," Brenda said.

Shay tried to pull away from Brenda, to look her in the face, but Brenda wouldn't let go.

"I thought he wanted to date me, but really, he just wanted me to be a fuck partner for him and his friend."

Shay tried to pull away again. Brenda still wouldn't let her.

"Just listen, Shay," Brenda said, holding her. "It feels easier this way."

"Okay," Shay said, holding her friend.

"You remember when you were joking on my machine and you asked if that was me you saw leaving T and A's that morning?"

Shay nodded.

"Well, it was. It was one of my first nights stripping."

"Stripping? Brenda—"

"Don't judge me, Shay. I really wanted to do it. I really loved doing it, but I am in so much trouble now." Brenda finally let go of Shay and allowed her to look at her.

When Shay looked into her eyes, she could see that everything Brenda had said was true.

"Can we sit down?" Shay asked, noticing the slight scratches on both sides of Brenda's face.

"Yeah."

They both sat down on the beige couch. Even though Shay currently had the pole at her house, she could tell Brenda had moved her furniture around to accommodate the pole.

"I'm sorry, Brenda." Shay grabbed her hand.

Brenda took her free hand and wiped her face. Snot was about to drip from her nose. "I don't know what to do. I don't even know how to look at this. I agreed to have sex with him in the club, and then when his friend joined in, I said no."

Shay didn't know what to say.

Brenda looked Shay in the eyes, then wiped her nose on the collar of her gown. She wanted to tell Shay the rest, but she couldn't bring herself to.

Shay leaned back. "Wow, Brenda, this is a lot."

"I'm in so much shit." She shook her head. "If I go to my captain, I'll get suspended for conduct unbecoming an officer."

Shay squeezed her hand. "This is a lot to figure out, Brenda, and you will, but are you okay?"

"I'm okay." She sucked the snot back into her nose. "I've just been reading a lot the last couple of days. I froze the evidence."

"I think we should call Shaundra. She's at Paul's house, and Karina is probably already asleep, but we should wake her up."

"They're going to think I'm stupid, Shay. I don't want to go through that. I can't take any more."

"We're your friends, Brenda. We've been together too long for that. I'm calling."

43

We spent the night in Brenda's living room. Brenda got the couch. Shaundra and I grabbed the pillows from Brenda's bed and spare blankets and camped out on the floor. Karina brought her own sleeping bag.

I faced the three-paneled mirror and leaned my back against the couch Brenda was sitting on. These were my junior high school girls. My dogs. My family. Shaundra, Karina, Brenda, and I were all the same in so many ways, but yet and still, we were so different. Innocence had been taken from all of us. In my opinion, Brenda was the last one to have it, and now it had been taken from her as well. Growing up, I had been so concerned about *getting grown*, that I forgot that the bigger part of the journey was to keep the inside of myself childlike.

We sat around the whole night and most of the morning. We took short catnaps, but not once were all of us asleep at the same time. This was a vigil of sorts. A shut-in for the wounded of heart. Shaundra popped popcorn the old-school way, in a pot with hot oil, then sprinkled it with cayenne, garlic, and a shitload of butter. The butter was soothing. *Heathen holy oil,* I thought to myself.

"I've been thinking," Karina said. The bowl of popcorn had just been passed around for the third time. Karina handed it to Shaundra. "Leaving here wouldn't be the worst thing in the world." Karina's legs were folded Indian-style, and a paper towel square with popcorn on top sat in the concave space between her legs.

She hadn't looked at us when she made this comment. She just kinda dropped it off into our universe and kept eating her popcorn.

"You thinking about going somewhere?" I asked finally. A part of me wasn't even sure I wanted to know. I was so exhausted from all the change happening in my life already.

"You know, you always think of things like that and either you jump up and do it one day or you don't." She popped a kernel into her mouth.

I thought about the fact that Karina always carried travel magazines around with her. Funny thing, I had never thought about leaving. I was envious that the possibility existed for her.

Brenda groped the decorative pillow in her lap. "That doesn't sound bad at all right about now. Being anywhere else might be good."

I nodded. We all nodded, but I knew what Brenda was feeling. At least I thought I did. I knew that moving wasn't going to make it go away. You can't move away from yourself. If I hadn't figured out anything else, that much I knew.

"I know the guy," Brenda said, not looking up. She focused all of her attention on the carpet right in front of her feet. She'd said it low, almost like she hoped we wouldn't hear her.

"What?" Shaundra said in the same low voice. "Who are you talking about?"

"The guy," Brenda said. "The guy who did this to me with Bruce. I know who he is."

Shaundra let her hands come up to her forehead. "Oh, baby. I'm so sorry."

I touched Brenda's leg. She didn't jump. "From where, Brenda?"

She brushed past me and headed into her bedroom. Karina, Shaundra, and I looked at each other. I could tell Karina was saying a silent prayer under her breath. Brenda came back with a photograph and handed it to me. It was her academy graduation photo.

"He's an officer?" I asked, shaking my head and looking up at her.

Her blank expression told it all.

"Jesus have mercy," Karina said, looking up to the ceiling.

I grabbed Brenda's hand and held it tight. "So he knows who you are?" I asked.

Brenda shook her head no. "It all seemed so out of place, I just froze. If I had said I was an officer, I don't know what would have happened, and if I would have said his name, that would have freaked him out. I just didn't say anything at first. It was a lose-lose situation. How can I go to my captain? How would that sound? I was moonlighting as a stripper."

I closed my eyes and held her hand yet tighter.

"I just can't believe it," she said. "We went through the academy together. Our badges were signed by the same person—Chief Clarborne. My only saving grace is that I switched branches when I became a bailiff. But if I go forward, I'm still going to be screwed. I was in the wrong too."

"It's going to be okay, Brenda," Karina said. "I know it is. Many people have done worse than this." She reached over and tapped Brenda's leg.

"Yeah," Shaundra said, joining the bandwagon.

I didn't know what to say. Everything seemed so big and weighted. I did what I'd been doing a lot of lately; I went straight into avoidance mode. That was the only strength I felt I had at the time.

"Y'all remember our last sleepover when we were kids?" I asked, feigning excitement. "It was right here in this living room. Actually most of the furniture is still the same."

"Shut up," Brenda said, trying to play along.

Shaundra was lying on her side now, her eyes barely open. "That was during your 'I love Darius' phase. 'Darius this. Darius that.' I remember telling you to screw him and get it over with."

I smirked. It seemed like the atmosphere was lightening up. I was tempted to throw a piece of popcorn at Shaundra. "I did screw him. See what you started? You liked that boy Brian, didn't you? The one who played on the junior varsity football team with the big ol' head."

"Don't get personal, Shay. I wanted to marry that boy." She lifted her head up from the pillow and smiled. "Anyway, his head wasn't *that* big . . . it was misshaped."

"Whatever," I said, laughing. I still didn't know what to do for Brenda. Karina started talking about Sammy Henderson, a boy from ROTC she had liked back in the day. I found myself thinking about Darius again. We were magical together. He got my body like no else ever had. Then, in that moment of deep thought, two things slapped me in the face. In all my years of living, despite how grown and fast I tried to be growing up, Darius and Marcus were the only two men I had ever been with. The other realization, though amazing, wasn't a shock to me at all. I was still in love with Darius.

"You're right," Brenda said soberly. "Most everything in here is still the same except for the couch and the strip pole when it's my rotation."

I clicked back in. Something told me to join Brenda on the couch. I flipped the pink thermal blanket off my legs and crawled up.

"Brenda, when it's all said and done, I want you to know that I am proud of you. You made a decision and stuck with it." I looked her in the eye. Her face was tired. "God knows I would have tried to stop you had I known you were going to do it, but I'm amazed at you. You became a real bona fide stripper. Big Mardi Gras. The girl shaking her thang with the feather mask on. Whoop-whoop." I smiled, then turned serious again. "What they did was wrong. Don't beat yourself up over shit that's in someone else's head. Just decide what you want to do about it."

Karina and Shaundra were quiet, but I could feel their presence.

Her eyes broke the slightest tear. "I'm afraid. I don't know what to do."

I hugged her face to mine. "I can't say my situation is the same, but I don't know what I'm going to do about Marcus. Or Darius. Shaundra doesn't know what she's going to do about Brandi." I glanced at Karina. "Karina doesn't know if she wants to move. But you know what? We're still here. And we're still together, and that says a lot." Shaundra grabbed my leg and Karina inched off her sleeping bag closer to the couch. Our bond gave me peace. Whatever happened next, whatever Brenda decided, whatever we all decided, we would handle it together.

Acknowledgments

To my agent, Jim Levine—thank you for all that you do. Every girl should be so lucky. To the LGLA family, I appreciate all of you. To Malaika Adero, you are bad-ass! Thank you for seeing the vision and supporting this series. To Judith Curr, Krishan Trotman, my publicist, Sybil Pincus, Robert Legault, and everyone at Atria—thank you for being a part of my team!

For everyone else I'd like to thank, I asked them to come up with a stripper, let-loose-and-express-yourself alter ego—of course it was easier for some than for others:

To M. Dizzle, Nickie Lola, Officer Good-n-Plenty, RJ, Vanessa, Chestie D, DJ, Jiggles, Fantasia, Sir Touch-A-Lot, Lala, Shay, and Supernatural—thank you for your love, encouragement, and support. To my mother, sisters, and brothers—I love you. To my dear father-ancestor-spirit—I'm a daddy's girl to my heart; your love and guidance is active in my life. Jah!

To African-American booksellers—thank you for having this book on your shelves. To Gabrielle/Aphrodite SNP—let's have some fun! To my readers—thank you, thank you, thank you for picking this up. I hope you join me for the next book in the series, and if you have an idea for a reading/event in your area, let me know! And don't forget to join us for a *Girls' Nite Out!* Love ya!

Visit www.kimonajaye.com.

About the Author

Kimona Jaye is an agent for a New York literary agency. Yes, she does own a pole.